Just as she felt herself ~~~~~~~ ~~~~~~~~~ ~~~~ ~~~~ I distinctly heard a voice saying 'I shouldn't bother to scream. There is nobody to hear you.'

As soon as she walks into the old Tudor mansion, Elly senses that something is wrong, that the house itself is hostile towards her. But why should it hate her when she'd never been there before? Then strange things start happening to her—she hears ghostly singing, sees people in the woods dressed in old-fashioned clothes, and hears threatening voices in the house.

And then she learns that the skeleton of a girl, dressed in red velvet, was found in an old chest in one of the bedrooms. She decides to try to solve the ancient mystery, but in digging up the distant past she uncovers secrets about her own family history which will have a lasting effect on her whole future.

Carol Hedges was born in Hertfordshire and after university, where she gained a BA (Hons) in English Literature, she trained as a children's librarian. She has had various jobs including running her own children's clothes business, being a secretary, a dinner lady, and a classroom assistant at a special needs school. Later she retrained as an English and Media teacher. In 1999 she gave up full time work to concentrate on her writing. She has had four books published and a short story broadcast on the radio. *Red Velvet* is her second novel for Oxford University Press.

Red Velvet

Other books by Carol Hedges

Jigsaw

Red Velvet

Carol Hedges

OXFORD
UNIVERSITY PRESS

OXFORD
UNIVERSITY PRESS

Great Clarendon Street, Oxford OX2 6DP

Oxford University Press is a department of the University of Oxford.
It furthers the University's objective of excellence in research, scholarship,
and education by publishing worldwide in

Oxford New York

Athens Auckland Bangkok Bogotá Buenos Aires Cape Town
Chennai Dar es Salaam Delhi Florence Hong Kong Istanbul Karachi
Kolkata Kuala Lumpur Madrid Melbourne Mexico City Mumbai
Nairobi Paris São Paulo Shanghai Singapore Taipei Tokyo Toronto Warsaw
and associated companies in Berlin Ibadan

Oxford is a registered trade mark of Oxford University Press
in the UK and in certain other countries

First published 2001
First published in this paperback edition 2002

Database right Oxford University Press (maker)

British Library Cataloguing in Publication Data available

ISBN 0 19 275191 3

1 3 5 7 9 10 8 6 4 2

Typeset by AFS Image Setters Ltd, Glasgow

Printed in Great Britain by
Cox & Wyman Ltd, Reading, Berkshire

To everything there is a season, and a time to every
   purpose under the heaven:
A time to be born and a time to die . . . A time to kill
   and a time to heal . . .
A time to love and a time to hate; a time of war and a
   time of peace.

Ecclesiastes 3:1–8

The restorer found it. He was working in an upstairs room, replacing rotten skirting boards. He stumbled across it in a corner. A large oak chest, the leather straps that bound it crumbling with age. He dragged it out onto the landing, shouting down to the others to come and see what he had discovered. Mrs Morton came too. After all, it was still her house. Until the last bit of work was complete. Then the National Trust, to whom she'd sold it, would move themselves in and herself out.

'Got yourself something interesting there, Shaun?' asked one of the men.

'Don't know,' Shaun replied, kneeling to blow the dust off the top of the chest.

'It's an old clothes press,' Mrs Morton said. She bent down and ran a finger gently along the edge of the lid. 'Lovely carving,' she murmured. 'Seventeenth century. Original too. I don't remember seeing it before, but then, the house has got into such a state. I don't really know what might be lurking up here.'

'Wonder what's inside,' Shaun remarked. He looked sideways at Mrs Morton, his glance taking in her shabby summer dress and unravelling espadrilles. Must be down on her luck, he thought, having to sell the family house. 'Could be treasure, maybe?' he suggested hopefully. 'Lost family fortune? Then you'd be able to keep the old place.'

Mrs Morton smiled drily. She'd long given up hope of

finding a fortune. 'Open it up, Shaun,' she said. 'Let's see what riches await me.'

Shaun heaved at the heavy oak lid. 'Blimey, it weighs a ton,' he puffed. 'Hang on, just get my fingers under the lid; here it comes.'

With a loud creak, the ancient wrought-iron hinges finally gave way and the lid lifted.

A cloud of acrid-smelling grey dust rose up from inside the chest, causing everyone to stand back. They coughed and wiped their eyes. Then, re-gathering, they stared expectantly down into the chest.

There was a long silence.

The figure lay bent double, knees drawn up to its chin. One arm was wedged between its body and the side of the chest, the other arm appeared to be trapped underneath.

The body must have lain there for many hundreds of years, for the flesh had rotted away, leaving only yellow-white bones and scraps of ragged material to bear witness that this had once been a human being. The skull was tilted upwards, as if the eyeless sockets were still searching for a last chink of friendly daylight before the lid closed down; jaws gaping wide to draw in one last precious breath of fresh air.

'Oh my God!' one of the men whispered. He turned his head away.

Shaun whipped out his handkerchief and held it to his mouth. A third workman made a retching noise. Only Mrs Morton remained unmoved, staring with strange intensity at the recumbent figure.

'Poor thing,' she said quietly.

Shaun took the handkerchief from his mouth. 'Shall I call the police?' he whispered shakily.

Mrs Morton looked at his blanched, terrified face. 'The police?' she said gently. 'I think it's a little late for that, don't you?' She reached down and softly touched the frayed and ragged material.

'Red velvet,' she murmured. 'Look—do you see? She was wearing a red velvet dress.'

1

'I heard a girl singing last night,' Elly remarked.

She buttered a second slice of toast. Back home, she never ate breakfast, trading it for an extra fifteen minutes in bed, but today she felt hungry. Must be because she hadn't slept in her own bed.

'I doubt it,' her mum said doubtfully. 'You probably heard somebody's radio. Sound can carry a long way in the country.'

'It *wasn't* a radio,' Elly answered. 'It was a girl. She was singing in the woods.'

Her mum shrugged. 'Well, I'm not going to argue with you. If you say that's what you heard, then I believe you.'

Elly cut the toast into quarters. She bit into one piece, slipping the rest to Flossy under the table.

'Stop feeding that greedy dog,' her mum scolded. 'I can see what you're both up to.'

She picked up Elly's plate and put it in the sink. 'Listen, I have to go into the village this morning. I've got to see about Aunt Rose's pension and return her library books. And we really should get some more dog food. There's only a couple of tins in her larder. Do you want to come?'

Elly shrugged. 'Suits me,' she said. 'Do you think there'll be any decent shops?'

'Not what *you'd* call decent. It's only a tiny village. But if you like, we'll go into town later on next week. There's a brand new shopping centre opened up.' Her mum paused. 'I can hang on until you've washed your hair,' she said pointedly. 'And I don't suppose you'd fancy wearing something else rather than those tatty jeans, would you?'

Elly pulled a face. Since when had her mum joined the style police? She got up, sighing.

'Maybe I won't come,' she muttered.

Her mum pressed her lips together. 'Suit yourself,' she said. 'Only I thought you said yesterday you'd like a look round the village.'

'I'll think about it, OK.'

'Well, don't take all morning making up your mind.'

Elly went up to her room—a small back bedroom that looked out over the garden and beyond to some woods that ran the length of the row of cottages. The room contained a narrow bed covered with a flowered bedspread, a basket chair, and a wooden chest of drawers with an oval mirror framed in dark wood. No pictures, no carpet. The floorboards were sanded smooth and polished. Standing on the threshold, Elly got the impression, even though her things lay strewn around, that nobody had slept there for a long time. The room felt solitary. It was used to keeping itself to itself.

She opened the window and leaned out, resting her elbows on the sill. She looked across the garden to the woods. She *had* heard a girl singing, she thought rebelliously. What did her mum know? She stilled herself, listening . . . Absolute silence. She hadn't heard a car going by all morning. It was like being in another time zone. Pale shafts of spring sunlight slanted across her arms—it was going to be a perfect May day. Elly glanced down at her watch: 9.35. In the real world, she would be in French. Mayday, mayday—wasn't that French for 'help me'?

But this wasn't the real world, she reminded herself,

6

and she wasn't in school. She was here, in this meagrely furnished bedroom in somebody else's house. Aunt Rose's house—whoever Aunt Rose was. Elly couldn't remember either of her parents ever mentioning her before. And now Aunt Rose was in hospital and they were temporarily looking after her house and minding her dog.

Elly sighed. Too many things were happening. Too quickly. It was becoming harder to stay in control. She got up. Peered at her reflection in the mirror. Pale pointy face, large dark eyes, and a mass of frizzy hair. The startled hamster look. Elly ran her fingers through her hair. It felt dry and brittle. Black candyfloss. Too bad, she wasn't going to wash it. She tied a Gap bandana round her head. It would have to do for now. She leaned forward, examined her chin. Shit! The Himalayan mountain range of spots was still there. Still, nobody she knew was going to see. That was the best thing about being here: nobody could see her, nobody could get at her.

'Are you coming or what?' her mum shouted up the stairs.

'All right!' Elly shouted. 'Don't stress. I'm coming, OK.'

It was a one-street village. The shops, small and housed in crooked old buildings with red-tiled roofs, wound their way down from the Morton Arms pub to the war memorial on the green. They passed a small fish'n'chip shop, a saddler's, and a chemist before discovering the post office. It doubled as a general store and sold everything from dog biscuits to clothes pegs. Elly wandered round listlessly picking things off the shelves and putting them back. Her mum shopped. Outside, Flossy lay full length across the narrow pavement, head on paws, causing havoc amongst the shoppers.

7

Why had it all started to go wrong? Elly mused. She knew things had been OK once. Good times with friends. Feeling secure. Now they were not, and she was not. That was why, after the phone call, when her mum told her the news about Aunt Rose, her heart had lifted with the sudden joy of realizing that she could escape, get away. Even if it was only for a while. That was the real reason she had begged to come with her. Told her that nobody did any real work after SATS. Said she could take time off, no problem. Assured her the school wouldn't mind. Elly remembered holding her breath, crossing her fingers, praying that her mum would agree. Now, even though she knew it was mean, she couldn't help feeling glad that Aunt Rose had fallen sick. She hoped the illness would last a long time. That way she could stay here and feel safe.

Elly picked up a packet of plastic bottle stoppers shaped like fruit. Who on earth bought this stuff? She put it back on the shelf. This was getting boring. She went to find her mum in the checkout queue. 'I'll go and untie Flossy, all right?' she told her.

Outside, the dog had found a friend. She was lying on her back, still in the centre of the pavement, paws and tongue lolling, whilst a boy was petting her. He looked up. 'Nice dog,' he said approvingly. 'What's her name?'

'Umm . . . Flossy,' Elly told him.

'I like spaniels.' The boy stood up and smiled. 'They always look like they've just heard a really good joke!'

Elly eyed the boy, carrying out a running inventory in her head. He seemed about her age, maybe a bit older, she thought. Nice looking too—bleached-blond hair and blue eyes. She wished that she'd listened to her mum's advice and put on her better pair of jeans, the ones with fewer rips. Washed her hair, maybe used some concealer.

'You on holiday?' the boy asked.

'Just visiting,' Elly said.

8

'Thought I hadn't seen you around here. Staying long?'

'Err . . . no,' Elly mumbled. She stared down at her feet. The boy waited politely for her to continue. Elly wasn't used to one-on-ones with good-looking boys. She wished she could think of something witty to say, but her brain refused to co-operate. Fortunately, her mum chose this moment to come out of the shop.

'Ah, there you are,' she said. 'Ready to go?'

Elly nodded. She bent and untied Flossy. The boy watched her.

'Bye, Flossy,' he said. Then he looked straight at Elly. 'See you around, maybe?'

'Err . . . maybe,' Elly said, vaguely. She didn't want to commit herself. After all, they'd only just arrived. Best to be cautious. No point in getting into something she might regret later on. She pulled the reluctant dog to its feet and walked away.

'Well,' her mum remarked cheerfully as they threaded their way along the narrow pavement back to the car park, 'I turn my back on you for one minute and you're already attracting attention.'

'What do you mean?'

'I was just commenting on the nice young man.'

'So?'

'So I'm pleased you've made a friend, that's all. No need to snap my head off.'

'I don't have friends.'

'Oh, Elly!'

'Well, I don't,' Elly muttered, falling into step behind her. 'Believe me, I don't.'

' "*Morton House*",' Elly's mum read aloud from the leaflet she'd picked up in the village post office. ' "*A typical Tudor*

9

house built in 1540 for the Morton family, wool merchants of the staple of Calais.'' Sounds interesting, doesn't it?'

'Uh-huh.' Elly lounged in an armchair trying to find something to watch on TV. It was after lunch. Her mother had rung the hospital and checked on the unknown aunt's progress, arranged to visit later on. Elly flicked from one channel to another. A bee fumbled drowsily against the window pane. Flossy stretched out by the empty hearth. This was her second day with her temporary owners. They'd fed her. She was adapting.

'I thought we might go and look round this afternoon?' Elly's mother continued.

'Huh?'

'Morton House.'

'Do what?'

'Elly—have you been listening to a word I've said?'

Reluctantly, Elly dragged her eyes away from the TV screen where teams of overweight housewives were attempting to fill supermarket trolleys, cheered on by a manic audience. Who on earth watched this crap?

'Yeah, I heard every word, Mum,' she lied.

'Good. And it will help your history.'

Oh great, Elly thought, changing channels again. She'd just agreed to something educational. Bad move.

The afternoon sun beat down on the roof of the car as Elly and her mum scoured the car park looking for a bit of shade. Morton House (Open Tuesday to Sunday, 10–5. Coach Parties by Arrangement) could just be glimpsed through the trees. It was a two-storey house, the walls lime-washed white, crisscrossed by exposed black timber beams. There were roof tiles the colour of sun-dried tomatoes and marmalade, lines of twisty red brick chimneys.

In the back of the car, the dog panted and whined dolefully, trying to force her head through the half-open window. Poor thing, Elly thought sympathetically, knowing how she felt. Her clothes were sticking to the vinyl car seat.

'Right,' her mum said firmly. 'I think we'll put the car here. It's in the shade and you can come and get Flossy after we've looked round the house.'

'I could always stay here with her while you look round,' Elly suggested hopefully.

'She'll survive,' her mum said. 'She's got a bowl of water, and we'll leave all the windows open a bit.'

'But she might get overheated,' Elly persisted. 'She might suffocate and die.'

'I promise you she won't suffocate and she won't die.'

'Perhaps I should stay and mind her?' Elly tried again.

Her mum sighed. 'I thought you wanted to look round.'

'Umm . . . I'm not really bothered,' Elly admitted.

'Well, I am. You can't mooch around all day. Come on, it's not a big house. It won't take long.'

Reluctantly, Elly unpeeled her body from the front seat and got out of the car. Historic houses were OK but no big deal. She glanced down at her watch. Perhaps if they whizzed round this one really fast, she might be able to return and rescue the dog. And herself.

'This is the great hall, where they held banquets and dances.' Her mum had bought a guide book at the entrance. She read details from the first page. 'Rather magnificent, isn't it?'

'Is it?' Elly looked around. Dark oak panelling, small windows that didn't let in much daylight, stone floor, and lots of musty old tapestries showing hunting scenes.

Hardly magnificent, she thought to herself. She shuddered. There was something unfriendly about this room. It felt hostile and unwelcoming, as if it didn't want her to be here.

'It's cold,' she muttered.

'They didn't have central heating in the sixteenth century.'

They passed out of the great hall and followed the arrows pointing the way up the wide wooden staircase. Her mum continued to read from the booklet as they went. *'Staircase by Matthew Fairfax, a local craftsman,'* she read. Elly ran her finger along the carved newel posts and wondered why she felt so ill at ease. It was almost as if the house didn't like her. But that was absurd, she told herself. Houses didn't have feelings! But the sensation would not leave her alone. And it was getting stronger all the time.

'The portraits up the Great Staircase represent four hundred years of the Morton family,' her mum read. Elly looked at the portraits. Paintings in heavy gold frames. Round ones. Oval ones. Large square ones. Stiff, unsmiling people who all seemed to be called Hugh or Anne. They wore ruffs and uncomfortable looking clothes. Boring, Elly thought. Like looking at somebody's photograph album.

'Look,' her mum stopped in front of one picture. 'Now, doesn't he remind you of somebody?'

Elly peered at the portrait. 'No,' she said.

'Oh. Only I thought he looked a bit like that boy you were speaking to this morning.'

'Oh, *Mum*, get real!'

'Sorry. Only joking.'

They reached the top of the stairs and came out onto a long gallery with five or six rooms leading off it. There were objects in glass cases at the far end. A couple of middle-aged ladies wearing sashes that said 'guide' on them were standing about chatting to visitors.

The windows of the gallery looked out onto the back of the house. Elly saw flower beds full of roses and herbs, a round pond with a fountain in the middle, and what looked like a small maze over to the left. Flossy would like to explore that, she thought to herself wistfully. So would she. It was too nice a day to be stuck inside this old house.

Elly stood at the far end of the gallery, wondering how a house with so many windows could seem so dark and menacing. She shivered. It was almost as if the windows were trying to keep the sunshine out rather than letting it in.

'Come and see this,' her mum suddenly called. She was bending over a wooden box. Its lid was raised. Elly could see that it had a round hole surrounded by padded material.

'What is it?' she asked.

'A close-stool!' her mum said triumphantly. 'I bet you don't know what it was used for.' Elly dutifully shook her head. Her mother enjoyed explaining things to her. Sometimes it was easier just to play along. 'Early portable toilet—see, you put a chamber pot inside the box and sit on it.'

'Eughh! That is totally gross!' Elly wrinkled up her nose in disgust.

'You wouldn't survive two minutes in those times, would you?' her mum laughed. 'No central heating, no proper toilets, no TV.'

'I wouldn't have minded this bed though,' Elly muttered. They had wandered into one of the rooms off the gallery. In the centre was a large four-poster bed, surrounded by primrose-yellow silk curtains. It had a matching silk coverlet and was piled up with silk cushions. Elly grinned. This was more like it, she thought. She could picture herself lolling amongst those cushions, with her CD player, sketch pad, and a plate of chocolate biscuits, the curtains closed against the world outside.

At the foot of the bed was a large oak chest and Elly sat down on it, hoping that none of the guides would notice what she was doing. She was beginning to feel tired. Idly, she poked her fingers into the carved leaves and spirals that decorated the sides of the lid, enjoying the smooth, cool feel of the wood under her fingers. Her mum walked about the room, exploring all the objects, reading all the labels. She was obviously enjoying herself, Elly thought. Her mum liked looking round old places. Elly could take them or leave them. Give her a good shopping mall any day.

Sighing, Elly glanced down at her watch. Maybe she could sneak out for a breath of fresh air, she thought. She would need one soon; it was getting very hot and stuffy. She wiped her sweaty forehead with the back of her hand and wondered why she was finding it so hard to breathe. And then, suddenly, she felt a tightness in her chest, just as if some giant hands were trying to squeeze all the air out of her lungs. She started gasping for breath. There was a roaring sound in her ears, the room began to spin wildly around her.

'Elly! What is it?' Her mum was by her side in an instant, pulling her to her feet. Fortunately, as soon as she stood up, the giddiness stopped. Elly found she could breathe normally again.

'What happened?' her mum asked, peering anxiously into her face.

'I don't know. I think I just felt faint or something.'

'Perhaps you'd better go out and get some fresh air.'

'OK,' Elly agreed. 'Give me the keys, I'll check on Flossy.'

Her mum opened her bag, handed over the keys. She was still looking worried.

'Are you sure you feel all right now?'

'Yeah, I feel perfectly fine,' Elly said. 'Don't make a fuss. Look, I'll see you by the pond in the garden. Take your time. Enjoy looking round. I'll be OK, really.'

Elly turned and ran back downstairs, pushing past the visitors coming in. She had to get outside into the fresh air. She had to get away from the claustrophobic feeling that had followed her ever since she entered Morton House. Most of all, she had to escape from that hot, stifling room. At last she stood on the steps of the house, gulping in the sweet spring air. Something very strange had just happened to her. She'd never known herself to faint before. But it was more than that: just as she'd felt herself losing consciousness, Elly had distinctly heard a voice saying: *'I shouldn't bother to scream. There is nobody to hear you!'*

2

Elly sat on the edge of the pond, watching fat orange fish circle aimlessly round and round. The water was so clear and blue that it looked as if they were swimming through the sky.

In the centre of the pond, a chubby stone Cupid holding a conch shell poured out a melodious stream of tinkling water. Flossy lay at her feet on the grass, occasionally raising her head to snap at imaginary flies. The sweet smell of lavender and rosemary wafted over the wall from the scented garden.

Elly stared into the blue water. Stress. It must be stress, she decided. She was stressed. That was why she had felt so peculiar, nearly fainted, heard the strange voice. Out here, in the sunshine, it seemed rational. A logical explanation. She decided to forget the whole thing. She had imagined it. It hadn't happened.

A shadow fell across the grass. She looked up quickly, expecting to see her mum, but to her surprise, it was the boy she'd met in the village that morning. Elly glared up at him. He was the last person she expected to see, even wanted to see right now.

'Are you following me?' she snapped, saying the first thing that came into her head, as usual, and instantly regretting it.

'Hey, don't be so paranoid.' The boy squatted down by Flossy and began to stroke her long ears. 'I live round here.' He rolled the spaniel over and stroked her stomach. Elly felt herself un-tensing. She had to learn to be less

16

hostile, she told herself fiercely. This boy was only trying to be friendly. She must remember that she was not in school. This was not the prelude to another one of Jessica's little games. 'Sorry,' she said, 'I didn't mean to snap, I was thinking and you startled me.'

'No problem,' the boy said. 'I could see you were miles away. I shouldn't have crept up on you like that.' He smiled. 'Look, let's start again, OK? Hi, how're you doing, my name's Hugh Morton.'

'Elly Laverty,' Elly replied. Then the penny dropped. She stared at him. Hugh Morton—the boy had the same name as the portraits. As the place itself.

'I see you've worked it out,' Hugh said. 'That's right: Hugh Morton, as in yes-I've-got-the-same-name-as-the-House.'

'You own this place?' Elly was impressed.

'We used to.' Hugh sat down beside her. The dog instantly tried to get onto his lap. 'It belonged to my family for centuries. It doesn't now. Last year, my gran sold it to the National Trust. Now we only own one of the cottages. You probably passed it on your way here.'

Elly gazed at the boy, open mouthed in astonishment. Somehow, she'd just assumed he was a local boy from the village. So her mother was right. She scrutinized him carefully. Made the connection. He looked like the paintings in the house. Same fair hair, straight nose, grey-blue eyes. It was uncanny. Stick a lacy white ruff round his neck, Elly thought, and he could have stepped straight out of one of the family portraits. Funny she hadn't noticed. Suddenly, Elly realized that she had been staring at the boy for some time without saying anything. She was being rude. Hastily she lowered her eyes.

'Er . . . yeah, so why did your gran sell the house?' she asked quickly, to break the silence and cover her embarrassment.

17

'Death duties.' Hugh Morton settled himself more comfortably on the grass. He seemed pleased to have the opportunity to talk. 'She had no choice. You see, when my grandfather died, there were complications over his will and she ended up in terrible debt. And then, the house was falling down—nobody had looked after it for ages. We're not very good at maintaining our family homes.'

'*Our family homes?*' Elly echoed in amazement. 'Jeez, how many have you got?'

Head on one side, Hugh considered her question. 'Well, there's the house in Normandy—that's where my parents live. My stepmother is French. And the London house— we rent that out to rich Arabs visiting London. And this one, which is the oldest. My father was really angry when Gran sold it. Really seriously angry. I don't think he'll ever forgive her. Selling off my inheritance, he said. I'm the only son, you see, so it should have gone to me. But I don't mind. At least they've done it up nicely. It was a terrible tip. In the end, poor old Gran was living in two downstairs rooms, with no proper running water because the drains had all packed up. And it was freezing cold in winter. I used to come and stay in the holidays and honestly, talk about down and out—it was dreadful! I'm sure it was affecting her health too. She's much better off in the cottage. And the way I see it, it was her decision, after all.'

Elly thought about this. 'Don't you *mind*?' she asked. 'I mean, having strangers tramping all over your house? Looking at your furniture and things? I would hate it.'

'Oh, a lot of the stuff in the house isn't ours,' Hugh said airily. 'They brought it down after the house was restored. It's *genuine*, of course, but it wasn't there from the beginning. There are some original pieces—the furniture upstairs belonged to the family. The stuff in the glass cases. The portraits, of course. Anyway, Gran made sure she took her favourite bits and pieces with her when she moved out. So it's not like it is her house any more.'

Elly nodded. She could see what he meant, though it still seemed rather sad. Giving up a house that had been in your family for centuries. Like being made homeless. She'd much rather have lived in Morton House than in a cottage.

'Did you enjoy looking round?' Hugh asked. 'Did you see the famous family ghost in the west wing?—Only joking!' he added, as Elly looked at him in alarm.

'It was very interesting,' Elly replied, a little stiffly. She wasn't quite sure how to take Hugh. One minute he was deadly serious, the next he was teasing her. And she'd never met anybody whose family actually owned three houses. He looked ordinary, but for all she knew, he might be a lord or something. She wasn't sure how you spoke to a lord.

All at once, she felt unsure of herself. 'Look, I'd better be off now,' she said, scrambling to her feet. She hauled on Flossy's lead. 'My mother will be wondering where I am.'

'See you again some time?' Hugh asked, looking up at her.

'Yeah,' Elly called back over her shoulder. 'See you.'

She set off towards the house. Her mum was standing on the terrace. Elly quickened her pace. She did not want the two of them to get chatting. Her mum would say something embarrassing. She could turn social embarrassment into an art form.

'Are you all right?' her mum greeted her.

'Fine,' Elly reassured her. 'I'm OK.'

She glanced back. Hugh Morton was still sitting by the

pond watching her. He waved. Elly managed a brief smile. She turned back to her mum.

'Let's go,' she said.

Elly could not stand hospitals—they always brought back vivid memories of sitting for hours in Casualty with a broken leg when she was eight. She hated watching patients being wheeled to and from the lift. Hospitals were full of pale dressing-gowned people shuffling slowly along the corridors. Like a lunatic asylum. And then there was The Smell. Hospitals freaked her out. She watched her mum get ready to visit Aunt Rose, glad she was staying in the house. So many things spooked her nowadays. Spiders, confined spaces, heights, silences . . . The list was getting longer all the time. Maybe *they* were right: maybe she was paranoid. She sat sideways in an armchair, legs sprawled over the arm, flicking through a magazine she'd bought in the village. Her mum picked up the car keys.

'I'll be back in a couple of hours.'

'Give Aunt Rose my best,' Elly said without looking up.

'I will.'

The front door slammed. There was the sound of the car spluttering into life and going down the lane. Then silence. Elly spent some time looking at the magazine, finally deciding that it was rubbish and a waste of her money. Then she glanced at her watch. Nothing on TV yet. She surveyed the room, mentally taking an inventory of everything in it. Plain white walls; two comfortable chairs covered in flowered chintz in front of the brown-tiled fireplace, rag rug, embroidered fire screen. Brass fire-irons, set of flowered plates on one wall. A small TV on a low wooden table and a pine bookcase stocked with Mills & Boon romances. Dog noisily asleep on the floor.

And then, all at once, something struck her as a bit odd. At home, they had loads of family photos—embarrassing ones of her as a baby; her parents on their wedding day. But here, there was nothing. Nothing on the mantelpiece; nothing on the TV or the bookshelf.

Strange, Elly thought. She'd never been in a house that was quite so impersonal. There were no ornaments, no bits and pieces. The house told her nothing about the individual who was supposed to live here, almost as if she didn't exist as a real person.

Elly was filled with curiosity. Who was this unknown woman—what did she look like? Did she have any family? And why was there nothing here to answer her questions? She got up and trailed upstairs in search of clues. She knew there was nothing in her room, she'd already made a thorough examination when they first arrived, so she opened the door to the other bedroom and went in. She was *not* snooping, she told herself, just checking the place out.

At first glance, there seemed nothing much worth checking out. A single bed with a peach coverlet, peach striped walls, little gold wall light above the bed. Elly opened the small pine wardrobe. Her mum's stuff was hung on one side, Aunt Rose's on the other. Aunt Rose's clothes consisted of old lady dresses, plain blouses, and boring tweedy skirts. Nothing interesting there.

Next she turned her attention to the chest of drawers. Nothing there either. Just underwear in the top drawer, neatly folded jumpers smelling of lavender and mothballs in the two below. Disappointed, she closed the bottom drawer. Then she noticed a small cane bedside cabinet. This looked slightly more promising. She crossed the room and was just about to open it when, suddenly, she froze. Outside in the wood, someone was singing. Elly recognized the song. So she'd been right. It was not a radio. For a fraction of a second, she hesitated, hand outstretched towards the cabinet door. Then she straightened up. The cabinet could wait. Right now, she had something else to check out.

Sunlight slanted through the oak leaves, dancing in the air and dappling the path before her with sunbeams. Elly walked quickly on, pausing every now and then to check that she was still going in the direction of the voice. There was a sudden rustling in the undergrowth and a couple of deer crossed the path. Deer? She must have misjudged the extent of the wood. From her window, it looked no more than a small green slice of trees between the road and the back of Morton House. But she'd been walking for some time, and she still hadn't reached the perimeter. And the wood seemed to be getting denser, trees taller and more thickly crowded together, their branches forming an arch over her head, like a long, high-roofed green tunnel.

At the end of the tunnel, the path broadened out into a clearing. There was a cottage. A low, thatched primitive-looking building. Smoke poured from the chimney and there was a small wooden lean-to on one side.

Elly stopped at the edge of the clearing. Who on earth would want to live in this out-of-the-way place? New-age hippies? Weirdos? Nutters? She sniffed. The place smelt. A piggy, unwashed, smoky smell. It was then that she saw the girl. She was sitting in front of the cottage on a low stool, singing to herself. Her hair was hidden under a white linen cap, like a baby's bonnet. She wore a long brown dress, filthy around the bottom and covered by a white apron.

A weirdo, Elly thought. She was right. Good voice though. The girl was grinding something in a bowl, and singing, her voice rising sweetly and clearly into the smoke-filled air:

22

> *'Greensleeves was all my joy*
> *Greensleeves was my delight*
> *Greensleeves was my heart of gold*
> *And who but my lady, Greensleeves.'*

Brown frizzy tendrils of hair framed the girl's round, tanned cheeks. She had dark brown eyes, a snub nose, and a wide red mouth. The face of somebody who'd spent all her life outside in the fresh air. All at once, the girl stopped working. She sat very still, listening to something, her head on one side. Then she stared with a fixed intensity along the path that led away from the cottage. Elly saw the colour suddenly flood into her cheeks. She hurriedly bent over her work again, grinding whatever it was with a desperate, almost feverish, energy. The next minute, a boy on a bay horse rode into the clearing. He dismounted, walked over to the girl and bowed low, taking off his wide-brimmed black hat as he did so. Elly looked at the boy. Her jaw dropped open in surprise—it was Hugh Morton. But what on earth was he doing in a place like this?

3

Elly felt an unexpected stab of jealousy. But a second glance showed her that this boy could not by any stretch of the imagination be the same Hugh Morton that she'd met at the House. There was a strong family resemblance—same blue eyes, same-shaped face. But this boy was slimmer, his features more delicate. He moved gently, smoothly, almost like a girl disguised as a boy. And his clothes! Elly could not see Hugh Morton wearing the stuff this boy had on: bright leaf-green coat and knee breeches, both decorated with bunches of green satin ribbons, white shirt with a stiff lace-edged collar and frilly lace cuffs, fawn leather riding boots, and the wide-brimmed black hat, with white ostrich plumes. He looked, Elly thought, grinning to herself, like some character out of a history textbook.

'Good day, Eleanor,' the boy said. He seemed slightly ill at ease. He stood awkwardly looking down at the girl and fiddling with his hat brim. His hair was exactly the same colour as Hugh's, fair and streaked by the sun, but curled down onto his shoulders in long ringlets.

Elly stared in fascination. Who were these two people, she wondered, and what on earth was going on here?

The girl barely looked up in response to the greeting, but her colour intensified until her cheeks were practically beetroot. 'Good day, Hugh,' she murmured, carefully setting down her bowl on the ground and keeping her eyes on her lap.

'What? Not look me in the face? Why, Eleanor, what

24

does this mean? After all, haven't we known each other from childhood?'

The girl continued to stare at an imaginary spot between her knees. 'But we are no longer children,' she said quietly.

'All the more reason for us to be friends now,' the boy replied, 'remembering what we once were to each other.'

At this, the girl raised her head and looked, not at him, but along the path from which he'd just ridden. 'And does your gracious mother rejoice to have you back?' she asked coolly.

'My "gracious mother" as you call her, is pleased to see me returned safe and well, yes, and sends a message to say that she hopes to see you up at the house soon.'

'Please tell her she is most kind to remember me,' the girl replied awkwardly.

'Oh, *Eleanor*.' The boy squatted down beside her, so that his face was level with hers.

The girl instantly turned her face away so that she couldn't see him. The boy put out a hand and tried to hold on to one of her hands which were clasped so tightly together in her lap, but the girl was too quick for him and snatched it away.

'What is it?' the boy asked, his face a picture of woe. 'Why are you acting like this? I—'

But before he could say another word, there was a rustling sound in the bracken. The boy jumped to his feet guiltily and sprang back as the bushes parted and a second girl stepped out into the clearing.

'So *here* you are, brother!' the girl exclaimed loudly as she strode towards him. 'Do you know I have walked an *age* all over the park to seek you out!'

She was beautiful. Her hair was ash blonde, and hung in thick ringlets down her back. A few stray ringlets curled around a face of exquisite loveliness: small and heart-shaped with huge periwinkle-blue eyes, a tiny straight nose, and a small, delicate rosebud mouth. Her skin was creamy-white, with just a faint petal-pink flush on her cheeks. She had on a dress of crimson silk that shimmered in the pale afternoon sunlight. Round her shoulders was draped a delicate muslin shawl, which made her long swan-like white neck look almost luminous. The contrast with homely Eleanor could not be greater. It was like comparing a bright exotic butterfly with a dull, ordinary brown moth.

'Oh, Arbella, you do exaggerate things.' Hugh smiled fondly at her. 'Why I left you at the house not ten minutes ago. As I recall, you had your hand in a dish of sweetmeats.'

The beautiful girl pouted. 'Well, maybe that was so, but what are sweetmeats compared with the company and conversation of my beloved brother. Whom I have not seen for nearly a twelvemonth!' And she tossed her head, making her ringlets dance.

Suddenly, the girl stopped. She appeared to notice for the first time that she and her brother were not alone.

'Why, Hugh,' she said, raising her delicate winged eyebrows and opening her blue eyes very wide in surprise, 'who is this poor cottage girl?'

Elly saw Hugh turn red and his mouth tighten as he replied sharply, 'It is Eleanor Fairfax, sister. Surely you recognized her? Your dear friend Eleanor, who meant so much to you when you were growing up. You cannot have forgotten Eleanor, can you?'

By the look on Arbella's face, it was clear that she had indeed forgotten. She examined Eleanor curiously from head to toe, her glance taking in everything, from her ugly cotton cap to the hem of her dirty brown dress. 'Why, so it is Eleanor,' she drawled, 'but she looks so . . . different.'

Poor Eleanor, Elly thought. The country girl blushed and lowered her eyes in embarrassment.

'That is because Eleanor has had to work hard since you last saw her,' Hugh told his sister gently. 'Whilst you enjoyed yourself in London and Paris visiting the Court and seeing all the sights, Eleanor has had to keep house for her father. Did you not know that her mother died of the fever?'

Arbella stared at Hugh. Then at Eleanor. Her glance was shrewd and calculating. Finally, she seemed to make up her mind. Smiling sweetly, she went towards Eleanor, holding out her hands. Elly noticed, however, that her eyes were not smiling, and that she soon dropped Eleanor's hands and wiped her own furtively on the back of her dress when she thought nobody was looking at her.

'Dear, dear Eleanor,' Arbella cooed, 'I am rejoiced to see you again after all this time. How are you?'

'I am well, Arbella, thank you,' Eleanor answered politely. 'It has been a long time indeed.'

'Far too long,' Hugh added, 'for when we last met, we were all children and these woods and the park were all our playground.'

'And now look at us—here we are all grown up,' Arbella spoke gaily. 'I have been in France and London, learning how to be a young lady of fashion.'

'Speaking two languages,' Hugh added proudly, smiling at her.

'Speaking two languages, as you say, and you, dearest brother, have been in Oxford, learning how to be a successful man of letters. And Eleanor . . . ?' Arbella paused, faltered, a frown creasing her perfect white forehead.

'Eleanor is still our dear friend,' Hugh put in quickly, glancing at Eleanor who had taken no part in the conversation at all, reduced to looking from one to another, as if watching a game of tennis. 'Is not that so, dearest sister?'

'Of *course*.' Arbella nodded her flowery head. 'Of course it is so, and you *will* come up to the house very soon, won't you, dear Eleanor? I have some lovely jewels and several beautiful new dresses, made in Paris especially for me by the finest dressmakers. I'm sure you are *wild* to see them, aren't you!'

'Yes, Arbella,' Eleanor replied tonelessly but Arbella seemed not to notice her lack of enthusiasm as she smirked complacently and twirled round, to show off the shimmery silk dress.

'Well, that is settled then,' Arbella went on carelessly, waving her hand. It was clear that she had tired of Eleanor Fairfax and of their conversation. 'And now, brother, we must return to the house, for it is getting late and our mother will be anxious. And as I am *so* tired, you will have to let me ride.' She picked her way delicately across the grass to the horse, gathering up her long dress, and swung herself gracefully onto its back.

'Come, brother,' she commanded, settling herself more comfortably on the saddle. She rearranged the silken folds of her skirt. She ignored Eleanor, not even bothering to say goodbye. Hugh looked at Eleanor and shrugged his shoulders apologetically.

'Farewell, dear Eleanor,' he said softly. 'Until our next meeting.'

'God save you, Hugh,' the girl replied quietly.

They left. Arbella sitting sideways upon the horse, her fair curls bobbing rhythmically up and down on her shoulders in time to its footsteps, her brother walking alongside her. And although Hugh looked back wistfully several times, his sister never once turned her head.

For several minutes after they had passed from her sight, Eleanor Fairfax sat very still, her eyes fixed longingly on the path that led back to the house. Then she sighed and brushed some imaginary bits off her apron. She picked up the mortar and resumed grinding. After a few seconds, she began to sing again, softly but with heart-wrenching sadness.

> *'Greensleeves is all my joy*
> *Greensleeves is my delight*
> *Greensleeves is my heart of gold*
> *And who but my lord in his Greensleeves.'*

Elly stayed at the edge of the clearing watching until Hugh and his sister had gone. Then she made her way back through the wood. She'd realized that the three people were actors. You often saw people in historical costumes hanging around old houses re-enacting some significant event from the past. It was supposed to make it look more authentic. They must have been rehearsing some scene to play out in front of the coachloads of tourists that would come to visit during the next few weeks. They were probably living in the cottage. She only hoped it was better on the inside than the outside.

Elly wished now that she'd paid more attention when she and her mum had visited Morton House. She should have looked at all those portraits properly. Tried to read the guide book herself rather than relying on her mum for edited highlights. Then she might have understood what the actors were on about. It was obviously something important. They were good though, she thought to herself. Very good. The way the man bore such a striking resemblance to the real Hugh Morton. And the relationship between the two girls. The look of scornful disgust on the fair one's face. The humiliation in the other one's eyes. Completely authentic. It reminded her of

29

herself and Jessica Thornton. That first time, when it had all started. And Elly breathed in sharply, feeling the familiar pain in her chest.

4

L ooking back, Elly couldn't remember noticing Jessica Thornton much. They'd drifted along in the same class fairly amicably, had their own set of friends. What she could remember, with complete clarity, was the day they became enemies.

It was morning break. Elly was washing her hands in the girls' toilet. The door opened. Jessica and her little gang entered. Elly went over to the dryer, started waving her hands underneath it. Jessica sniffed, flicked her smooth dark hair, pulled a face.

'Ugh!!' she announced. 'It smells in here.' She shot Elly a quick glance. 'It's a sm . . . elly lavatory!' she repeated, drawing out the words as she spoke to make her true meaning quite clear. 'Very sm . . . elly!'

Her friends laughed. Jessica repeated the joke. More laughter.

'Way to go, sm . . . elly!' Jessica went on.

Elly turned round. Jessica pinched her nose. The gang copied her. For a moment, Elly didn't understand. This had nothing to do with her. Then she looked into Jessica's eyes which were like weapons and realization dawned. Red faced, she stumbled to the door. Laughter followed her out into the corridor. That evening, Elly tried to make sense out of what had happened. Jessica Thornton had never gone for her before. Nobody ever did. She was popular, well-liked. At least, she thought she was. It must have been an accident, she decided. She'd misheard, got it wrong. She blanked out the hostility in Jessica's eyes.

31

Nothing happened for a couple of days. Then Jessica struck again. This time Elly was left in no doubt of her intentions. They were waiting in line outside the Science lab when Jessica suddenly barged into her, sending her books and pencil case flying. Elly bent down to collect her belongings. Jessica, apologizing loudly, bent to help her. When Elly checked her possessions, her Parker pen was missing. She'd only just got it, a fourteenth birthday present from her father. After the lesson, whilst everybody was packing up, Elly went over to Jessica.

'Did you pick up my pen?'

Jessica stared at her blankly. 'No,' she said. Elly glanced down. The pen was lying on top of Jessica's folder.

'Um . . . I think you have it there,' she said.

'Excuse me?'

'My pen. That's it there.'

'That's mine,' Jessica said firmly.

Elly held her ground. 'I don't think so.'

She reached out for the pen. Like lightning, Jessica snatched it up.

'What are you saying?' she exclaimed loudly. 'I *stole* your pen? Is that what you're saying—that I'm a *thief*?' She glared at Elly. 'This is my pen. I've had it since last term.' She turned to the two girls sitting on either side of her, 'That's right, isn't it?' They both nodded. Elly bit her lip. She didn't know what to do.

'Is there a problem here?' the science teacher asked, coming over.

'Ask *her*!!' Jessica gathered up her books, her back ramrod straight, and stalked indignantly out of the lab. Her two friends followed her. Elly was left staring after them, not knowing whether to laugh or cry.

Why me? It was a question Elly asked herself frequently over the next few months. She had done nothing to annoy

32

Jessica. But the question remained unanswered. For some spiteful reason of her own, Jessica had decided to pick on Elly. And there was nothing she could do to stop her. For Jessica was clever. She played little games. Whatever happened, she always managed to make out that everything was Elly's fault. Coke spilled on her homework—Elly had knocked her elbow. Jessica's missing Geography book 'appeared' in Elly's bag. Jessica's ankle hurt—Elly had tripped her in PE. Her friends put it about that Jessica was the victim, Elly the bully. And though Elly constantly pleaded her innocence, Jessica managed to persuade everyone that Elly was making it up. In the end, even her own so-called friends. They started drifting away. Putting distance between them. Elly was weird, Jessica said, paranoid. She was strange, different. You only had to look at her. Elly needed counselling. She, Jessica, was telling the truth. Her popularity grew. Elly's declined. It was like a see-saw. Once Elly was up up, now she was down down.

Elly didn't know how to handle it. She'd never been unpopular, disliked. She couldn't tell anybody—not that she would, because she had no proof. It was her word against Jessica's. And Jessica's ever-widening circle of friends. It was like living in a looking-glass world where black was white and right was wrong. And it went on and on, week after week. Elly tried not to show her fear, kept it hidden inside, but it lapped up into her eyes for all to see. Eventually, she lost confidence, stopped believing in herself. She moved to a safe space inside her head. Stayed there, didn't speak. She went around with her head down, making no eye-contact. It was a way to survive.

The memories of that time had not faded, were still crystal clear in her mind. Seeing the actors had triggered off everything all over again. That night, Elly dreamed that she was being chased down a long corridor by Jessica and her gang. The old nightmare returning to haunt her. She felt her heart pounding in her chest, fear giving wings to her feet as she ran. She awoke in the early hours, sweat pouring off her, finding it hard to breathe, feeling as if she'd been stifled. For a long time, she lay absolutely still, watching the dawn rise, trying to get her head around what her life had become. Subconsciously, she knew she was going to have to go back and get it sorted. But how? What could she do?

The Sunday morning sun filtered through the kitchen blind. Elly sipped apple juice. Her mum and Flossy had gone for a Sunday morning walk. Her mum had never been keen on dogs but the little spaniel was doing her best to win her round.

Today would be a good time to read that guide book Elly thought. Find out more about Morton House. She knew her mum was planning to spend time at the hospital when she got back from walking the dog. Fine. Being on her own didn't worry her. It was so quiet and peaceful here. She would get the book and do some sketching. She'd brought a sketch pad with her. She wanted to draw the actors while they were fresh in her memory.

Elly decided to take her sketchbook out into the garden. She settled down on the grass and opened up the Morton House guide book. She flicked through, closed it again, pulled a face. She was not interested in reading about the actual house, the amount of work it had taken to restore it. What she really wanted were family details. And there was nothing interesting. Nothing at all about Hugh and Arbella. Still, that was no problem, she knew what they looked like.

Elly drew. She paused every now and then, held the drawing away from her, studied it, then continued. It was a talent, her art. Everybody said so. Some day, if she got the grades, Elly hoped to go to art college, be a professional artist. Over the last few months, drawing was the one thing that had kept her sane. Art therapy. When things had started to get bad, she would shut herself in her room and draw. Immerse herself in her work and try to forget that there was a world outside and it didn't like her.

Elly drew on. She had no notion of time passing. She didn't sense someone creeping up behind her. It was only when she heard a gasp that she realized she was being watched. She whirled round, slamming the pad shut. Hugh Morton was standing behind her. Elly swore loudly.

'For God's sake! Why do you keep doing that?' she exclaimed.

Hugh looked embarrassed. 'Sorry,' he apologized. 'Your mother said it would be OK.'

Flustered, Elly scrambled to her feet. 'My mother? Where is she? What are you doing here?'

'Hey, chill. I met your mum walking Flossy in the woods.'

And she asked you back, Elly finished silently. My mother, the interferer. Great. Thanks, Mum!

'Look, sorry to startle you. Again,' Hugh said. 'Can I look at your drawing?'

Elly's inclination said no. Her art was private. But her curiosity got the better of her. Perhaps Hugh could shed some light on the scene she'd seen acted out. She handed him the sketch pad. 'It's not very good,' she murmured. 'I haven't finished it yet.'

Hugh flipped open the pad. He stared at Elly's work. Then he raised his eyes and looked at her, a puzzled frown on his face. 'It's Arbella Morton, isn't it? And Hugh. But I don't understand—how did you do this?'

'Just drew it.'

'I mean, where did you see a picture of them? There aren't any portraits in the house. My gran has the only pictures of them and she keeps them locked away for safety.'

'The actors,' Elly told him. 'I copied them.'

'I'm sorry?'

'I saw them rehearsing yesterday in the woods and . . . ' Elly tailed off.

Hugh was staring at her with a strange expression on his face. 'What on earth are you talking about?' he asked. Elly glanced at him wondering if he was teasing her again but Hugh was deadly serious. He wasn't joking this time. 'I've never heard of any actors,' he said, shaking his head. 'Is this some sort of wind up?'

'Nice one, Mum,' Elly said, sarcastically. 'You didn't have to ask him back, did you?'

'I felt sorry for him,' Elly's mum said.

'*Sorry!* Why on earth?'

'I think he's a bit lonely.'

'Mum, boys don't get lonely,' Elly told her. 'They find another boy to hang out with. Fact of life. How many times have you seen one boy going around on his own? Almost never. They always go around in twos or threes.'

'Not Hugh,' Elly's mother said. 'Did you know he's recovering from glandular fever?'

'No.'

'That's why he's staying with his gran. His parents live in France. And I think, reading between the lines, they're too busy to make much time for him.'

'Right.' How did her mum know all this? She must have been questioning him all the way back. Honestly,

Elly thought wryly, if they ever made interrogation an Olympic sport, her mum could do it for England.

'He spends all his holidays here in England. When he's not at boarding school. Not much of a life, is it?'

'I suppose not,' Elly admitted.

'Hugh says the kids in the village are not very friendly—they see him as an outsider because he belongs to the Morton family and doesn't go to the local secondary school.'

'Right.' Elly could relate to that—she was an outsider. Not by choice either.

'That was a funny thing about your drawing, wasn't it?' her mum said, abruptly changing the subject.

'Coincidence.'

'How could you have drawn a girl and a boy from a picture you'd never seen?'

'Stranger things happen. It's no big deal.'

'What was that about actors?'

'I was just kidding around. You know, winding him up a bit.'

Elly avoided eye contact. She'd managed to bluff her way around the actors. Lucky for her Hugh didn't know her well enough to tell when she was lying through her teeth. Her mum sometimes knew even before she opened her mouth.

'You are going to go and meet Hugh's gran this afternoon, aren't you?' Elly's mother continued. 'I thought it was very nice of him to invite you.'

'I might,' Elly replied cautiously.

'Oh, Elly! You said you would. And you promised that you'd take your sketchbook and show her your drawing.'

Elly lay on her bed in the tiny, white bedroom, staring up at the ceiling. She was finding it very hard to get a grip on reality. She had assumed that the three people she'd seen in the woods were actors, rehearsing a scene to perform for the tourists. Now, she realized they weren't.

So who were they? Elly felt a sudden shiver of fear run down her spine. *You know who they are*, a voice inside her answered. She shook her head. It couldn't be true. It didn't happen in real life. Certainly not to people like her. And yet the more she tried to block it out, the more the conviction persisted. Either she had completely lost the plot and was having hallucinations, or she really had seen three people from the past. She had heard them speaking. And it had felt just as if it had taken place in her own time.

'Elly?' her mum called. 'I can give you a lift if you're ready now.'

'I'm coming.' Elly got off the bed. She gave herself a quick glance in the mirror, pulled a face at her reflection and picked up her sketchbook.

5

'Hugh and Arbella Morton,' Helen Morton said. Her voice lingered lovingly on the two names. 'They were twins, you know.'

'Really?' Elly leaned forward in her chair.

They were sitting outside in the walled garden at the back of the cottage. Hugh had placed a white picnic table and three chairs in the shade of a small tulip tree. Helen Morton picked up the delicate white china teapot and poured tea into three rose-sprigged bone-china cups. Everything was so elegant, Elly thought. Tiny home-made scones, triangular crustless sandwiches, cakes on a silver three-tiered cake stand. It was like being in another age, when meals were something to be eaten at leisure and savoured. Elly sighed as she poured milk into her tea. Heaven! There was even a tiny pair of silver tongs to pick up the sugar lumps.

She sipped her drink, glancing covertly over the top of her cup at Helen Morton. She must have been very beautiful when she was younger. Clear blue eyes, thick silver-grey hair, and delicate features. She was wearing a navy cotton skirt and a white blouse with a delicate lace collar. Her hair was piled up on top of her head in a fluffy bun. She reminds me of Arbella, Elly realized with a shock of surprise. Fragile, like butterfly-wings.

'Yes, they were twins,' Helen Morton continued. She set the teapot carefully down on its stand. 'The only twins we've ever had in the Morton family, to my certain

39

knowledge. They were born in December, 1649, the youngest of six children.'

'Six?' Elly exclaimed.

'They went in for big families then. So many children died young, you see. The Mortons lost three children before their first birthdays, so it was vital to keep on having babies. They needed to ensure that the family line continued into the next generation.

'Hugh and Arbella's births are recorded in the family Bible. I think it must have been a wonderful thing—twin babies born alive and well. And at Christmas time too. Just when the year was at its coldest and most bleak. There was a great feast. They killed twelve sheep and ten pigs, you know. Everyone was invited to attend. It must have been quite a celebration, I think.'

'Then what happened to them?'

'They grew up here, in the House,' Helen Morton said. 'She was very beautiful, Arbella. Beautiful and a little spoilt. I suppose it was because she was the youngest. Her brother Hugh doted upon her. They were quite inseparable. He wrote to her nearly every day when he went away to Oxford. And she wrote back—she knew how to read and write. That was Anne Morton's doing. She always insisted that her daughters were educated alongside their brothers.

'Arbella wrote such amusing letters, all about her life in the countryside and her trips to London and to Paris to see the sights. All the Morton letters are preserved in the library up at the House.'

'Don't forget you promised to show Elly the pictures,' Hugh reminded her.

'So I did.' Helen Morton pushed back her chair. 'I'll go and get them now, whilst I remember.' She got up and walked a little stiffly into the house. 'Give Elly some more tea whilst I'm gone, Hugh dear,' she said over her shoulder as she passed his chair.

'She's nice,' Elly said approvingly.

Hugh looked fondly after the old lady. 'I think she's pretty special. She knows so much about the family. And in spite of everything that's happened to her, she never complains about anything.' He refilled her cup.

Helen Morton reappeared a few minutes later, carrying a small flat wooden box. 'Now then,' she said, beckoning Elly over. 'Come and see Hugh and Arbella Morton.' She opened the wooden lid.

There, resting on a bed of white silk, were two tiny oval portraits set in gold frames, like two exquisite jewels. Elly stared. Two pairs of deep blue eyes stared back. Two fair skinned, pink-cheeked faces. Two dainty smiling mouths. Two golden-haired children each looking as real and fresh as if their portraits had been painted yesterday.

'Wow!' Elly breathed.

'Aren't they lovely?' Helen Morton said softly. 'See how alike they were—I think they must have been ten or eleven when these pictures were painted. Miniatures, that's what they call these little portraits.' She smiled affectionately at the pictures. 'My pretty children. Far too precious to go on display.'

'Gran has a soft spot for Hugh and Arbella,' Hugh grinned.

'That's because they were twins. There's something special about twins. And they were so devoted to each other. Such innocents.'

'And because of what happened to them,' Hugh said. 'Tell her the rest of the story.'

Helen Morton sighed deeply. She looked down at the two fair faces, lying side by side on their silken beds. 'They disappeared,' she said sadly, 'just before their sixteenth birthday.'

Elly's eyes widened. The two figures she'd seen in the woods looked to be about sixteen years old.

'It was 1665, the year of the Great Plague,' Helen Morton continued. 'The family was staying in London at the time. They couldn't get away because of the disease. It must have been terrible. I don't think we can even begin to imagine it. Whole families shut up in their houses and just left to die. People dropping down in the streets. The stench of death everywhere. Plague carts rumbling round at night to collect the bodies. Such panic and fear. Nobody allowed out of the city in case they carried the infection with them.

'Quite soon after the family arrived, John Morton, the oldest son, fell ill. Then Hugh's wife Anne and then two of the youngest children. And of course, as soon as word got out of their plight, the whole family was locked into the house, and the plague officials painted a red cross on the door with the words "Lord have mercy upon us" above it. Nobody came near them. Nobody brought them any food or water. They were just left. Locked away in that hot, airless house, all windows sealed shut, slowly and agonizingly dying one by one.'

Elly shuddered. 'How awful.'

'There was no escape,' Helen Morton went on. 'The front door was locked from the outside and there was a watchman on duty day and night. But somehow, Hugh Morton, their father, managed to get word to his steward in Hertfordshire that he was going to try to smuggle Hugh and Arbella out of the city. They had not caught the plague but he knew that they would, if they stayed in that terrible house of death for any length of time. He sent word when to expect them. But they never arrived.'

'Maybe they died in the house with their parents and the rest of the family?'

'No, we know that they escaped,' Helen Morton said. 'The family was very rich and the deaths of rich people were recorded. They just vanished. Somewhere between

London and Morton House, Hugh and Arbella disappeared and nothing has ever been heard of them since.'

'Until last year,' Hugh interrupted. 'Tell her about the body, Gran.'

'Yes, the body.' Helen Morton's eyes were sad and faraway. 'Some workmen found it. In an old oak chest. The skeleton of a young woman in a red velvet dress.'

'Red was Arbella's favourite colour,' Hugh added.

'We had it looked at by a couple of experts and they told us it was probably the body of a young girl, aged maybe fifteen or sixteen, and that it dated from the seventeenth century.'

'So we know what happened to Arbella,' Hugh said. 'But we still don't know how she got there, do we, Gran?'

Helen Morton sighed, looked at the miniatures. 'They were such dreadful times,' she murmured. 'Everybody terrified of catching the plague. I think somebody in the village must have heard about the twins' return. They probably feared that they would bring the plague back with them. So they decided to kill them. What other reason could there be?'

'The money?' Hugh suggested.

'Yes, there was always the money. You see, Elly, Hugh Morton entrusted all the family jewels and money to Hugh and Arbella. He didn't want them falling into the wrong hands—there were so many thieves and looters on the prowl and they had been known to strip dead and dying bodies bare to find valuables. So maybe there was another motive after all.'

'But what about Hugh?' Elly asked.

'Nothing was ever heard of Hugh.' Helen Morton shook her head slowly. 'Probably murdered as well and left to rot in a ditch. Such a sad, sad end to two happy, carefree children who never meant any harm to anybody. Nothing went really right for the Morton family after the twins disappeared. It was as if the heart was ripped out. The house and land passed to distant cousins—my branch of the family, but it wasn't the same. Something vital and living died with those two innocent ones. It could never be revived.'

Helen Morton looked up at Elly and smiled sadly. 'I know Hugh laughs at me, Elly, but I firmly believe that whatever terrible thing happened all that time ago has left some kind of curse upon the Morton family.' She sighed, cradling the little box gently in her hands. 'Families. They all have their secrets, don't they?' she murmured. 'Their skeletons in the cupboard.'

'Except that we actually have a real skeleton,' Hugh said. 'Now, show Gran your drawing, Elly. Honestly, Gran, you must see this—it's the spitting image of Arbella. I don't know how she's done it since she's never set eyes on her before!'

Elly picked up her sketchbook and opened it up at her drawing of Arbella. 'It's not very good.'

Helen Morton bent over the page. 'But this is amazing,' she exclaimed. 'It's so like her. Older, of course—but the same expression, even the same colour dress. How can this be?'

'Umm . . . I think it's just me,' Elly said, casually. She'd had time to prepare an answer. 'I was copying one of the portraits in the house. I gave it a different dress. It probably looks like Arbella because all your family look alike, don't they. I mean, you look a bit like her too.'

Helen Morton laughed. 'Thank you for the compliment,' she said. 'Perhaps I did look a little like her once. My side of the family was distantly related to the Mortons. But it's still a lovely picture. You are good at drawing, aren't you!'

'I want to be an artist when I leave school,' Elly admitted.

'I can quite see why. You have real talent, doesn't she, Hugh?'

'Yeah, she's good,' Hugh agreed.

Elly felt her cheeks crimson. She wasn't used to so much praise. 'Umm. I think I'd better be getting back now,' she stammered in confusion, closing her sketchbook.

'Yes, of course,' Helen Morton said gently, sensing her nervousness. 'I wouldn't want to keep you if you have things to do. I really appreciate your coming over. Now, would you like to call your mother?'

'Actually, I thought I might walk back,' Elly said. 'My mum's probably still at the hospital.' She picked up her cup and saucer and placed it on her plate.

'Leave that, my dear,' Helen Morton said. 'You are our guest. Besides, I have a dishwasher.'

'Yes, it's called me,' Hugh said. 'Look, I'll walk back with you some of the way, if you like.'

'OK,' Elly agreed somewhat reluctantly. She stood up. Remembered her manners. 'Thank you for having me, Mrs Morton,' she said.

'Helen—it's Helen. And it's a pleasure,' Helen Morton smiled. 'Come and see me again, won't you. I don't get a lot of visitors.'

Elly nodded shyly.

'Ready?' Hugh said. 'We can cut through the park to the woods at the back of your house. It shouldn't take long.'

6

A curse on the Morton family. Elly echoed the words in her mind as she walked with Hugh across the green lawn. A curse. A curse. Maybe that explained why Morton House felt so cold and unwelcoming. Why Helen Morton had had to sell it. Why Hugh had glandular fever.

As if sensing her thoughts, Hugh said: 'You know, you really mustn't believe all that stuff about curses.'

'Oh, I don't know,' Elly countered. She recalled the way the windows of the house seemed to keep the daylight out rather than let it in. She remembered the voice in her ear. There was something wrong with that house. Something evil. She knew. She'd felt it.

Hugh shrugged. 'Well, sorry, but I don't believe in curses,' he declared. 'Or ghosts. It's all just superstition. Only don't say that to Gran, because she would be upset. She needs something to blame for the family misfortunes.'

Elly closed her mouth firmly. She was thinking about telling him what she'd experienced. The truth. Now, she decided she wouldn't. Hugh would only laugh. And she wanted him to think well of her.

They walked on in silence.

'She liked you,' Hugh said. 'I could tell. You'll have to visit her again.'

'I will,' Elly nodded.

'So how long are you staying?'

'Don't know. Week or so. Until Aunt Rose is better, I suppose.'

'Funny you never heard about her before.'

'Well, that's families for you,' Elly said in what she hoped was a 'don't ask me anything else' voice. They were approaching the edge of the woods. 'You don't mind living with your gran?' she asked to change the subject.

'It's OK,' Hugh replied. 'My parents are both very busy, you see. Even more so now the house has been sold. My father says he has to work extra hard to make up for everything we've lost through the sale.'

'He doesn't mind you living with her?'

'Oh no, it's not like there's a feud. He thinks it's her duty to look after me. After what she did, he says, it's the least she could do. But actually, I'd much rather be here than in Normandy, where my father and stepmother live. I have these two half-sisters,' Hugh pulled a face. 'As in: half-sisters, half werewolves. They are foul, both of them. There is nothing to do over there except keep out of everyone's way and I have to speak French all the time.'

'Il y a plus de mille élèves dans mon collège,' Elly said suddenly. They'd been doing about school in the French module last term.

'C'est vrai?' Hugh replied in perfect French, his eyes lighting up. *'Mais, tu parles français!'*

'Oh . . . no, not really,' Elly stuttered, scarlet in the face with embarrassment. Why on earth had she come out with that bit of French? She wasn't even aware that she'd learned it. She spent most French lessons at the back of the room, doodling on her pencil case and trying to blend with the furniture. She was useless at French. Once, she'd actually translated *'J'ai un chien'* as 'I've got a boyfriend'. It had taken her weeks to live that down! Inwardly, she cursed her mouth's ability to work independently from her brain.

'I'm not looking forward to going back to school,' Hugh went on, not noticing her embarrassment. 'I've got major exams next term.'

47

'Yeah, tough call,' Elly agreed. So Hugh must be older than her. She'd suspected he was. Maybe quite a bit older. Suddenly, all Elly's insecurities came flooding back. Hugh wouldn't want to hang out with her when he discovered she was barely fourteen, she thought. Add that to the fact that he went to a posh boarding school while she went to the local secondary school. Her family lived in a semi, his family owned houses. Lots of houses. One of them in France. And he obviously spoke French fluently. Hugh Morton inhabited a different world from her. Come on, who was she kidding, they had absolutely nothing in common. Face it, she told herself, however much she fancied him, it was a recipe for disaster.

'Er . . . look,' she said, hesitantly, 'you don't have to come any further, I'll be OK from here.'

'Are you sure?' Hugh said doubtfully.

'Yes.' Elly was more definite now. 'I'll see you around.' She clambered over the wooden style that separated the park from the woods. There was an awkward pause while she and Hugh stood on each side of the barrier.

'OK then.' Hugh looked puzzled.

'Right,' Elly said briskly. She waited an infinitesimal second to see if he'd suggest seeing her again. He didn't. 'Bye then,' she said.

'Bye.'

Elly turned and set off down the narrow path that led to the row of red-brick cottages. She sighed. Things had been going so well. Now she'd ruined everything. She'd been too abrupt and unfriendly. She knew it. Jumped to conclusions. After all, she had no proof that Hugh would drop her because she was younger than him. And he must have realized she didn't have the same background, but he'd never said anything about it. Why should he? He probably couldn't care less. She was the one with the problem. The stupid one. The one making A Big Deal out of nothing. She turned back, but it was too late, Hugh had gone. And she'd really hoped he would ask to see her again.

Cursing her stupidity, Elly walked on, kicking the dead leaves that lay in her path. Then all at once she stopped, stared down, a puzzled expression on her face. It was early summer. So why were there dead leaves piled up along either side of the path? Elly stood still. She looked up. Suddenly, without any prior warning, summer had given way to autumn. All around her, the leaves were falling fast, covering the woodland floor with a carpet of copper and russet-brown. A chill wind whipped through the bare branches of the trees and the air was moist and heavy with the rich decaying smell of autumn. What on earth was this? Elly wondered. An example of sudden and extremely local global warming?

Then, in the distance, she heard the sound of a horn being blown—three long blasts. Dogs barked and Elly felt the ground beneath her shake as a group of men and women on horseback suddenly appeared out of nowhere and thundered along the path, nearly knocking her over. Voices called out, harness jingled, and horses' breath rose in steamy clouds as they passed. Elly was just able to make out that the entire hunting party was dressed in the long, flowing clothes of the seventeenth century before they disappeared from sight as rapidly as they had come.

Elly stood motionless, waited. Perhaps there were more riders to come. Sure enough, a couple of seconds later she heard rustling in the dry bracken and the rhythmic sound of hooves. She flattened herself against an oak tree, but she need not have worried. Only two riders came cantering along the path this time: a boy dressed in black, riding a bay horse, followed by a girl in a long deep-red dress, neatly looped up over her saddle. She was riding a rather plump piebald pony.

49

Elly recognized the two of them.

'Oh, brother, is this not good sport!' Arbella Morton called out. Her cheeks were flushed with excitement, her long hair fell in damp ringlets. Elly could see great patches of sweat under the arms of her red cloth riding coat and across her slim back.

'I think we should walk the horses for a bit,' Hugh Morton responded. 'That pony of yours is not used to such exercise. Let him rest for a while. You don't want him to go lame.'

Arbella pulled a face. 'I don't want him *at all*,' she pouted. 'I wanted to ride the black mare with the white blaze, but father says she is too strong for me.'

'And so she is,' Hugh replied, dismounting and helping his sister off the pony's fat back. 'She goes like the wind, that black horse.'

'That is why she is the one for me!' Arbella exclaimed joyously. 'Every time I see her, I want to jump on her back and ride, ride to the end of the earth!'

'Oh yes? And what would you do when you reached the end of the earth?' Hugh smiled fondly at her.

Arbella looked at him slyly. 'Maybe we would find something quite wonderful. Chests of gold, silken dresses, wonderful jewels. Who knows? Perhaps we might meet the most beautiful girl in the world and bring her back for you to marry!'

Hugh went bright red. 'Don't tease, Arbella!'

'I am not teasing.' Arbella's eyebrows arched. 'I am only pointing out to you that the world is full of beautiful girls.'

'Like you?'

'Of course like me. And that some day, you will meet the right one for you.'

'Maybe I already have,' Hugh said thoughtfully. He looked sideways at her, then looked away.

Arbella groaned. 'If you mean who I think, no you have *not*,' she cried. 'Eleanor Fairfax is a *nice* girl, but she is plain and poor and most important of all, her family have become Dissenters.'

'Does that matter so very much?' Hugh asked.

'Oh, *Hugh*!' Arbella exclaimed. 'How can you say that! You have been away from home for so long that you know nothing. Have they no Dissenters in Oxford?'

Hugh shook his head.

'No?—Let me enlighten you.' Arbella took his arm. 'Eleanor's father, Matthew Fairfax, has left the true faith and is now leader of this sect. I heard the servants talking about it. Everybody in the village is talking about it. It is a disgrace. The sect are called Quakers, and they worship—if such it can be rightly called—in a house nearby. Hugh, they are terrible people. They believe that all men are equal. Do you not notice how Eleanor never addresses you as Master Hugh—nor me as Mistress Arbella? I tell you, it makes me wild. But that is how they are. They refuse to attend church on Sundays, or pay tithes. Oh, Hugh.' Arbella opened her eyes wide and looked pleadingly at Hugh. 'Hear me out, Hugh. You cannot, you simply *cannot* marry her.'

'But she is so sweet. And I feel so sorry for her. She is alone in that cottage now that all her brothers and sisters have married.'

'And her father is in prison, did you know that also?' Arbella cut in sharply. 'He is in Bedford jail for refusing to pay his taxes. He even dared to write a begging letter to our father asking him for assistance, but father wrote straight back and said his imprisonment was a punishment sent by God for deserting the true faith. As for Eleanor, she could easily go and live with one of her brothers if she chose.'

'But they both live in Amwell.'

'It is not half a day's journey from here.'

'But who would keep house for her father?'

'Oh, *Hugh*!' Arbella sighed. 'It is not love that you feel, it is pity.'

Hugh stared down at the ground, poking at the leaves with his whip.

'I speak the truth, don't I?' Arbella persisted.

'Perhaps. I don't know.'

'It is only because I love you as myself. It would break my heart to see you so mismatched.' There were real tears in Arbella's big blue eyes. They trickled down her cheeks as she spoke. 'Promise me, Hugh. Promise me you will never see her again?'

Hugh's face was equally a picture of misery. 'Oh, Arbella! You know I love you too. I would never do anything to hurt you, sweetest sister. If it means so very much to you . . .'

'Oh, it does. It does.' Arbella's lower lip was quivering.

'Then . . . I promise.'

Immediately, Arbella's tears turned to smiles. The change was dramatic. It was like the shock of sunshine breaking through a grey raincloud. She gave a little skip of glee. 'Then I promise in turn that I shall never scold you again,' she cried exultantly, giving his arm a squeeze. 'And now, please may we go home? I am getting so cold standing around in the wood.'

You bitch! Elly thought, as the sound of their horses' hooves faded away in the distance. Poor Eleanor Fairfax. She didn't stand a chance against Arbella. Her relationship with Hugh was doomed from the start. And Hugh Morton—wimp or what! 'Pretty children'—that was what Helen Morton had called them. Hugh was a child. But his sister . . . she was something else. Something far less innocent.

Elly continued back home. The path was now dry and clear of leaves on either side. The trees were thickly covered in green foliage. Autumn had given way once more to summer. She looked along the path to where she could see the cottage in the distance. Her mum was sitting in a deckchair reading the Sunday paper. Flossy was lying asleep beside her. Elly quickened her pace, reached the back gate. Unlatched it.

'Had a good time?' Her mum put down the paper.

Elly nodded. She propped her sketchbook against the deckchair and sat down next to the dog. 'Aunt Rose OK?'

'Not too good. They're going to do some tests.'

'Right.' Elly poked Flossy with the toe of her trainer.

'So what was Hugh's gran like?' her mum asked.

'Oh, you know, all right,' Elly replied vaguely.

'Did she like your drawing?'

'Yeah, she said it was good.'

'I thought we might go into town tomorrow,' her mum went on. 'There's the cathedral, some nice shops. Is that all right with you?'

Elly shrugged. 'Yeah, whatever.'

'Oh good. You're free. I wouldn't want to upset your arrangements.'

'What arrangements?' Elly stared up at her coolly.

'Oh well, you know, you might have made . . . plans.'

Elly rolled her eyes in an exaggerated way. 'No, mother dear, I am not seeing Hugh Morton tomorrow. If that's what you mean. Nor the next day. Nor any day after that.'

'Oh. That's a shame. I rather liked him.'

'Well, you see him then.'

'Elly!'

'He doesn't like me.'

'You always say that about everyone. I'm sure it's not true.'

'How would you know?' Elly snapped. Memories of school and Jessica's evil face came flooding back.

'Well, I like you.' Her mother smiled.

'Hooray,' Elly muttered.

'What makes you think Hugh doesn't like you?'

Elly shut her eyes. Why did her mum always want to know every detail about her life. Probe, probe. Question, question. It was like living with the frogging Spanish Inquisition.

'Just leave it, Mum, OK,' she said wearily. 'He doesn't like me. End of story.'

'Maybe you weren't very nice to him,' her mum persisted. 'You can be a bit prickly and snappy with people, you know. Perhaps you just gave him the wrong impression.'

This was so near the truth that Elly felt a stab of pain go through her. She pushed the dog roughly away, got up from the grass.

'Elly, are you listening?' her mum asked. 'I'm right, aren't I?'

Elly pulled a face, shrugged her shoulders.

Her mum sighed. 'And don't give me the confused teenager shrug,' she said.

'Well, stop treating me like a child then,' Elly shouted. Suddenly she hated her mum, hated everybody. She grabbed her stuff and ran into the house.

7

The kettle boiled, clicked itself off. Elly poured boiling water into the teapot. She checked the tray: toast keeping warm in a white linen napkin, butter, jam. Plate, knife, cup and saucer, milk in a jug, teaspoon. It only needed one more touch. She darted out into the garden and picked a fat apricot rosebud. Perfect.

'I've brought you breakfast in bed,' Elly announced, pushing her mum's door open with one foot. Flossy sneaked in ahead of her and parked herself by the side of the bed, ever optimistic.

'How nice!' Mrs Laverty sat up and reached for her glasses. 'What a treat. You can stay and keep me company,' she suggested as Elly carefully set down the tray in front of her.

Elly perched on the edge of the bed. Her mum poured tea, buttered a piece of toast. Elly watched as she ate. Her mum looked older, the lines on her face more pronounced. She must have slept badly, Elly thought guiltily. And it was all her fault.

After their row, Elly had stormed into the kitchen, grabbed a Coke and a packet of biscuits and gone straight to her room. She'd slammed the door, even though nobody would hear her. She hadn't come out again. Even the smell of bacon frying failed to tempt her. She'd stayed in her room, eating her way through the biscuits and drawing. It got dark. She drew on. She stopped only when her eyes felt as if they had rings of fire round them.

In the morning, she'd woken up, feeling calmer, more

55

like herself. She also felt slightly ashamed. She had overreacted. She lay in bed, wondering what to do to sort it. The idea of breakfast in bed suggested itself. She'd got up and crept downstairs.

Elly wished she was better at talking about her feelings. She was good at it once, but now the words wouldn't come. She'd lost the ability. And she seemed to have developed the habit of standing back and observing herself. As if she was no longer sure she knew who she really was. It was this feeling of detachment that had got her through the century-long days and weeks of bullying. But, of course, it wasn't bullying, was it, Elly thought grimly. Couldn't be. Because the school had an anti-bullying policy. Everyone knew it. They'd been told it often enough: 'We have a very successful anti-bullying policy operating. There is no bullying in this school.' It was trotted out at parents' evenings, assemblies, lessons. Yeah right. Trouble was, the people saying it never stood in the lunch queue, waited outside the school gate, hung out in the girls' toilets, or walked the corridors between lesson changes. Places where the 'anti-bullying policy' meant nothing. Meaningless words. The people who said it certainly weren't around when Jessica Thornton and her gang presented Elly with a home-made badge with 'Geek of the week' written on it. And then ran away from her, laughing. They weren't there the week after, when they gave her one with 'Fool of the school'. Nor when she got 'Nerd of the herd', followed shortly by 'A**e of the class.'

Elly sat pleating the edge of her mum's duvet cover between her fingers. It had been a nightmare. But she had survived. She remembered how she had managed it. Her strategy. She had created a wall in her head. Every day, she had added another layer, building it higher. Blocking out words that were not meaningless.

Her mum set the empty cup carefully on the tray. 'That was nice.'

Elly dragged her mind back to the present. She picked up the cup, poured more tea. 'Tell me about Aunt Rose,' she said encouragingly.

'What do you want to know?'

'Well, is she a real aunt? How come I've never heard of her before, that sort of thing. She's not very well off, is she?'

'How do you know that?'

'Well, she hasn't got much furniture. And there aren't any pictures or ornaments.'

'She only moved here recently.' Elly's mum moved the tray away. 'I suppose some of her things may be in storage.'

'Where did she move from?' Elly picked up the tray, placed it on the floor, where the dog examined it for scraps.

'A little village called Amwell. It's not too far from here.'

Elly frowned. She'd heard that name, quite recently too.

'Why did she move?'

Her mum sighed. 'Oh, Elly, I don't know. I suppose her old house got too big for her to manage.' She pushed the duvet aside briskly. 'Now then, I'd better get up if we want to go into town. Can you take the tray down for me. And feed Flossy whilst I have a bath.'

Elly picked up the tray, carried it down to the tiny old-fashioned kitchen. Her mum was being deliberately selective with information, she thought. She'd said practically nothing. But Elly had learned over the years that it wasn't what her mother said that was important, it

57

was what she left unsaid. The iceberg strategy. She only revealed the smallest amount. The greater part remained hidden. She'd inherited the same trait, that was how she recognized it.

Elly dumped the tray, started piling dishes into the sink. It was a strain being here on her own with her mum. Two people who found it hard to communicate at the best of times. Which this wasn't. She wished her dad was with them. But he was working abroad. His firm had offered him promotion, which meant him moving to Brussels. That was what she'd been told. He rang, sent e-mails, but she hadn't actually seen him for weeks. Elly however nursed a secret conviction that her parents were about to split up. She was continually waiting to be told that this was it. Final. No reconciliation. It scared her. She wanted to be told, dreaded being told. Quicksand. You could get sucked under.

Elly had witnessed so many people in her school going through their parents' divorces. She had seen their anger and pain. Even girls reputed to be hard had broken down and sobbed their eyes out in the girls' toilets when their parents had split up. She sighed. What was it about families, she wondered. Was it just her or did everyone hide behind walls in their heads? And why were there so many secrets? So many things that never got said?

'I bought this for you.' Elly's mum held out a paper bag.

They were having lunch in town. Thick home-made soup and crusty brown rolls. Blackcurrant cheesecake for dessert. Elly liked it here. The streets were old and winding. It had narrow passageways with overhanging buildings, which looked much the same as they probably did in the seventeenth century. The shops were good too, she'd treated herself to two T-shirts, an embroidered waistcoat, and a leather choker. She'd also bought a bunch of flowers for Helen Morton, to say thank you.

'You're spoiling me!' Elly dipped into the bag, found a tiny yellow oval-shaped box. 'What's this?'

'Open it.'

Elly opened the box, tipped the contents onto the table. Six tiny figures, each one no more than three centimetres high. They were dressed in bright scraps of wool and cloth.

'They're worry people,' her mum said. 'I bought them in that shop with the candles. They come from Guatemala. See, it says on the bit of paper in the box. When you have any worries, you tell them to the worry people. Then you put them under your pillow at night. By morning, the worry people have taken the worries away.'

If only it was that easy, Elly thought, sadly. 'Nice one, Mum. Thanks.' She re-packed the worry people into their box, slipped it into her pocket.

'So where to now?' she asked.

'Do you want to look round a bit more?'

'Could do.' Elly chased the last of her pudding round her plate. 'There's some good shops.'

'Yes. It's certainly changed a lot from when I remember it.'

'Oh?' Elly looked up, suddenly alert. 'You've been here before?'

'I used to come here sometimes when I was a child. Remember, I told you, I was born near here.'

'Really? You never said.'

'I'm sure I mentioned it in the car coming down.'

Elly replayed the conversation they'd had in the car. She vaguely remembered her mum saying something. Trouble was, she had been too buried in her own problems.

'So you knew Aunt Rose then?'

'A little.' Her mum started to gather her things.

'Only I'd have thought she'd have wanted to see her own family rather than us.'

'Ah well, beggars can't always be choosers,' her mum said lightly. She stood up. 'Right, if you've finished taking the pattern off that plate, let's pay and go.'

Elly followed her out. Her mum was being selective with information again. There was some mystery about Aunt Rose. She was sure of it now. Perhaps she had lost all her money. Or done something terrible that had cut her off from her nearest relatives. It was ironic, she thought, she seemed to know more about the Morton family, who meant nothing to her, than her own family who should mean everything.

Later that afternoon, Elly set off for Helen Morton's house. She was carrying the flowers. The dog accompanied her. Elly had not been sure about taking Flossy, but her mum had persuaded her: 'I'm sure Helen Morton will love to see her. Anyway, she needs an outing, she's been cooped up all morning.' So Elly had agreed, reluctantly. She did not know how Flossy would react if she encountered Hugh or Arbella on the way.

She need not have worried. Nothing unusual happened. Elly arrived at the cottage twenty minutes later having seen nothing more exciting than a coachload of tourists making their way up to the House. She'd managed to put Flossy's lead on her, but had not been able to part her from a large stick that she'd picked up in the wood.

Elly rang the bell, reminding herself firmly that she had only come to hand over the flowers. To say thank you to Helen. That was the sole reason for her visit. It didn't matter whether Hugh was in or not. She could live without seeing him.

'Sit!' she hissed at the dog as she heard somebody coming.

'Hello.' Helen Morton opened the door. 'For me? Thank you.' She bent down and solemnly took the stick that Flossy was offering her.

'Actually, these are for you,' Elly said shyly, holding out the flowers.

'Freesias! How lovely. And how kind of you to bring them, Elly. Come in for a bit—do you have time? Yes, of course that dear dog can come too!'

Helen Morton led the way into the neat blue-and-white tiled kitchen. 'Please, sit down,' she said. 'Now, I know I had a nice vase somewhere.' The spaniel placed herself next to Elly's chair, sitting very upright, on her best behaviour. Her brown eyes were fixed longingly on Helen Morton. Kitchens to Flossy meant only one thing.

Helen Morton filled a glass vase with warm water. She unwrapped the freesias. Today, she wore a baggy pair of jeans, a short-sleeved pink and white candy-striped cotton blouse. Her soft grey hair was pulled back in a French pleat. She's really, really nice, Elly thought. I wish she was my gran.

'Now then.' Helen Morton placed the vase of flowers on the table. 'Do you think that will do?'

Elly nodded.

'Would you like a drink? I expect you're a bit hot.'

'No, I'm fine,' Elly said. 'But I think Flossy might like some water.'

'Then of course she must have some. What a lovely dog. Is she yours?'

Elly explained the spaniel connection. Helen Morton found a suitable bowl and put a sheet of newspaper down on the kitchen floor. Flossy gratefully slurped up the water, managing to spread it onto the paper.

'Well now, Elly.' Helen Morton slipped into the seat

opposite. 'Hugh's not here at the moment. He likes to go up to the house to help out when they need him. But I'm expecting him back very shortly. And I know he'd be cross if I let you run away. He hasn't got many friends here.'

'He's better now, isn't he?' Elly asked. 'Mum told me he'd been ill.'

'Much better. You'd hardly believe the difference in him. When the school sent him home, he was barely able to walk. Poor Hugh.'

'I'd hate to be at boarding school.'

'It was his choice,' Helen Morton said. 'He didn't like the French schools. He wanted to board in England. His parents tried to dissuade him, but he made up his mind and he stuck to it. He can be very determined. It's a Morton family trait.'

'At least he's got you.'

'And I've got him.' Helen Morton smiled. 'It's nice for both of us. I don't see the rest of the family very much.'

Elly remembered Hugh telling her about the quarrel with his father. It seemed such a shame.

'And what about you, Elly?' Helen Morton continued. 'Do you have grandparents—I'm sure they must think a lot of you.'

'My dad comes from a big family; I see them quite a lot,' Elly told her. 'But Mum was an only child and her parents died before I was born.'

'Ah well, that's a shame. Families are important.' Helen Morton nodded. 'They give you a sense of your place in the world.'

'I'd like to know more about Mum's side of the family,' Elly said. 'But it's difficult trying to find out things.' Especially when nobody will tell you, she added silently.

'Maybe your aunt could fill in some of the background,' Helen Morton suggested.

'Yeah . . . maybe.' Elly wondered why this hadn't

occurred to her before. She'd only thought of finding information out about Aunt Rose. Not getting information from her. 'I might visit her when she's feeling better.'

'Good idea. I'm sure she'd like to see you. It's not every day one discovers an unknown niece!'

Or an unknown aunt, Elly mused thoughtfully. What on earth had Aunt Rose said or done? she wondered. Why hadn't she heard of her before now? There must have been a mammoth row. Maybe something really juicy and scandalous. It would be exciting to find out. So her family wasn't as posh as the Mortons. But that didn't mean they weren't as interesting.

'Well, Elly,' Helen Morton went on, 'would you like to stay for tea—I'm sure Hugh will be back any minute now.'

Elly glanced at her watch. She'd overstayed her time. 'I'd better go,' she said reluctantly getting to her feet. 'I'm supposed to be back soon.'

'What a shame,' Helen Morton said. 'Still, I'll tell Hugh he missed you. Perhaps you might like to call again. And please, will you feel free to bring Flossy?'

'I will,' Elly promised. She smiled at Helen Morton. Then, impulsively, gave her a hug. 'Thanks. Hugh's so lucky to have you.'

'Oh, I'm nothing special,' Helen Morton said. 'But I'm here if he needs me.'

Elly hurried back to the cottage, pausing only to drag Flossy out of some ditch where she had gone to ground. Her mind was full of schemes: finding a reason to see Hugh again; getting to the hospital without her mum knowing. She was so immersed in her schemes that she almost failed to see the two shadowy figures. The dog saw them though. She suddenly stopped dead in the centre of the path. Her nose pointed towards a little grove of trees. She crouched low, growling, the hair rising all along her backbone.

Elly followed her stare. There were two people in the shadows, almost merging into the trees. They were standing very close to each other, heads practically touching. She recognized them instantly. It was Hugh Morton and Eleanor Fairfax.

Elly saw that Hugh had got hold of one of Eleanor's hands and was murmuring something into her ear. She could not catch what he was saying, but she hardly needed to. Eleanor's blushing cheeks said it all far more eloquently than any words.

So Hugh Morton was sneaking around having secret meetings with Eleanor Fairfax. This couldn't have happened overnight. They must have been seeing each other for quite a while, behind both their families' backs. Elly watched Hugh raise Eleanor's hand to his lips, his long fair curls falling across his face as he gently kissed it. Eleanor lifted her face to his. Her eyes shone and her cheeks were flushed. For a moment, her face glowed with such happiness that she looked almost beautiful. Elly wondered whether Arbella knew what was going on. She hoped that she did not. Not quite yet. It would only be a matter of time before she did, though. Hugh Morton was too weak to keep up this level of secrecy. Elly was sure he would slip up sometime. Not that it mattered. Hugh was going to die anyway. Probably quite soon. And Arbella would be murdered, her body dumped in a wooden chest and left to rot. And Eleanor? Maybe she died too—of a broken heart.

That night, Elly had a strange dream. She was in a box. She was lying on her side, with her legs bent at the knee, her arms trapped beneath her. All around her, she could hear the worry people muttering away in some strange guttural language, but she could not see them because it was pitch dark. She could not move her arms or her legs either. It started to get hot in the box. Elly's face began to drip with sweat. It was falling into her eyes but she could not raise her hand to brush the drops away because her arms were pinned underneath her.

Long grey fingers of fear started to creep up her body. She began to panic. She tried desperately to free her arms so that she could lift the lid of the box. It's only a cardboard box, she kept telling herself as she struggled to pull one arm out from underneath her body. I can get out easily. But her arms were pinned so firmly that try as she might, she could not get them to move. One part of her brain was frantically thinking: *'No . . . no, must move . . . must escape before the air runs out.'* Another part of her brain kept telling her calmly: *'It's only a dream . . . only a dream.'*

And then she heard the voice again. At first it was only a faint whisper on the far edge of her consciousness, so quiet that she had to strain her ears to hear it. Gradually, it got louder and louder, until it drowned out the mutterings of the worry people. *'I shouldn't bother to scream,'* said the voice. *'There is nobody to hear you.'*

'But I recognize that voice!' the Elly in the dream gasped. 'I've heard it before. I know who it is.'

And then the screaming started.

Over and over again. Always the same word.

It sounded like a girl's name.

8

Elly opened her eyes.

Her mum was leaning over the bed, shaking her shoulder gently. 'Have you been having a nightmare?' she asked. 'Your bed is in a complete mess.'

Elly looked up into the familiar face. 'I had this awful dream,' she whispered. 'I was trapped in a box and I couldn't get out.'

'You poor thing!' Her mum sat on the edge of the bed, stroked Elly's forehead. 'I thought I heard you crying out in the night. But—you're very hot! And your cheeks are flushed.'

Elly tried to sit up, but sank back onto her pillow with a groan. 'I feel *awful*!' she moaned. 'My head hurts and I feel sick.'

'Oh, Elly! Don't tell me you're going to be ill.'

'Ill? I can't be ill!' Elly exclaimed. 'I was OK yesterday.'

'Maybe it's just a twenty-four hour thing,' her mum said. 'I'll get you some aspirin and a cold drink. Just lie quietly. I think you'd better stay in bed today.'

'Oh, Mum, do I *have* to?' Elly whimpered. She had plans.

'I'm so sorry. Hopefully it's nothing more than a chill. With a bit of luck you'll be up and about again in no time.'

Elly closed her eyes. The room was going round and round in a rather alarming manner. She felt hot, she felt awful. Tears of self-pity oozed from between her tightly closed eyelids.

The bedroom door slowly opened; Flossy's head appeared. She was licking her lips. Breakfast had obviously just happened. Elly patted the side of the duvet, then braced herself as the spaniel launched herself enthusiastically at the bed, landing clumsily on top of her. Flossy's sense of direction was nearly as bad as her own.

Elly put her arms around the dog and buried her hot face against the little spaniel's warm, biscuit-smelling side. 'It's not *fair*!' she whimpered. Flossy licked her cheek comfortingly. She turned herself round a couple of times and then settled down, wedging her bulk against Elly's side and giving a gusty sigh of contentment.

Her mum came in carrying a glass full of cloudy liquid and a mug. 'How are you feeling now?'

'I'm going to die.'

'Poor old you. Here you are: Disprins and some apple juice. Drink it all up and don't leave the bit at the bottom of the glass—I know you of old.'

Elly picked up the glass and, pulling an awful face, drank the cloudy liquid. She washed the nasty taste away with the apple juice. It was cool and refreshing. She stared blearily around the room. Everything seemed fuzzy. Her eyes wouldn't focus properly. Downstairs, the phone started ringing urgently.

'Back in a minute,' her mum said.

Elly took the worry people's yellow box from under her pillow and tipped them onto the bed. She hadn't really looked at them closely. She started sorting them into groups. Two of the worry people were dressed in red and looked so alike that she instantly christened them Hugh and Arbella. There was a mother and two little ones, she didn't know who they were, and the last one looked like Elvis Presley. Worry people—they could have been named after me, she thought gloomily. I'm a worry person. Elly picked the little people up carefully between thumb and index finger and placed them back in their box, just as her mum came into the room, looking anxious.

'That was the hospital,' she said, perching on the edge of Elly's bed. 'I'm afraid Aunt Rose has taken a turn for the worse during the night.'

'She's not going to . . . ' Elly let the words trail away.

'No, I shouldn't think so,' Mrs Laverty said quickly. 'Only the doctors are a bit concerned. I'll go in and see what's happened. Hospitals aren't the nicest of places, especially when you're old and on your own. And I know she misses Flossy.'

Elly screwed up her eyes and pulled a face. 'It feels like somebody's drilling a hole in my head,' she groaned.

Her mum placed a hand on Elly's forehead. 'You rest,' she said. 'I'll come and check on you at lunchtime.' She got up and went out of the bedroom.

Elly fell back into the bed. Her head hurt and her whole body ached. She shut her eyes and drifted into a deep and dreamless sleep.

The singing woke her. Drifting into her subconscious like wisps of smoke. Lifting her into consciousness. Elly opened her eyes and sat upright. Suddenly every nerve in her body was violin-string taut. She pushed back the duvet and stood up, swaying slightly. On automatic pilot, she put on her jeans and a top, slipped her feet into her trainers. At one level, she knew that she was too ill to get up, should lie down again, but the song drew her. It lured her, as if the notes of music formed an invisible thread linking her to the singer. She was being pulled towards the woods and she was powerless to resist.

Elly crept silently downstairs, went through the kitchen. The house was silent, empty. Her mum must have gone to the hospital. Flossy followed her to the back door, but Elly ignored the pleading brown eyes.

'Later,' she lied. She opened the door and slipped through. Walked quickly along the path through the woods until she recognized a familiar figure walking in the same direction ahead of her. Elly quickened her pace.

Eleanor Fairfax walked purposefully along the path that led to Morton House. She carried a covered rush basket over her right arm. As she walked, she sang, her voice echoing strangely in the silence that hung between the bare black winter trees. Her breath formed small white clouds in the chill air. She shivered and huddled more closely into her warm woollen shawl. A few paces behind her, Elly followed, her eyes never leaving the small, neat figure.

Eleanor Fairfax had made a real effort with her appearance. She wore a clean grey dress, the large brown woollen shawl wrapped around her arms and shoulders. Her head was covered by a white woollen cap with long ear-flaps. On her feet she wore stout leather shoes.

Swinging her basket, Eleanor made her way round to the back of the house until she came to the kitchen door. She paused for a second, screwing up her courage to go in. Then, she squared her shoulders, stuck her round, determined chin in the air and lifted the latch.

The kitchen was like a scene from hell. Girls in greasy aprons, their caps slipping off their heads, were rushing around carrying steaming pots and pans. A couple of young boys were turning a huge piece of meat on a spit in front of the fire, jumping out of the way as the hot fat spat upwards. The air was fragrant with the smell of spices and herbs, but so thick with smoke that it was difficult to see clearly from one end of the room to the other and the floor was slimy with spilt liquids and bits of rotting food.

Elly's eyes started watering. She wrinkled her nose in disgust, wondering how on earth the kitchen servants could stand it.

'God save all here,' Eleanor Fairfax remarked politely as she picked her way carefully across the hot, fetid room. There was a sudden silence. Everyone stopped what they were doing. The noise of busy chatter and friendly insults died away. All eyes turned to look at the intruder with her basket. Then turned from her to a huge woman in a filthy grey apron, standing at the table, putting the finishing garnish to a platter of fish. The woman had round, pebble grey eyes set rather too close together in a red puddingy face. She had thick lips, so that she rather resembled the fish she was arranging. She looked at Eleanor, her mouth set in a straight line of disapproval.

'What is your business here, Eleanor Fairfax?' she snapped.

Eleanor's shoulders went rigid. 'I have brought some embroidery to show Arbella. It is at her express wish that I come,' she said, forcing herself to hold her head high.

The cook wiped her nose on her filthy sleeve. Her sniff spoke volumes. '*Mistress* Arbella is in her room. I expect you can remember the way.' Her voice was cold, flat with dislike. Eleanor flinched as if she'd been struck. Then, regathering her poise, she dropped the fat cook a curtsy. 'I bid you good day,' she said, and scuttled across to the far side of the kitchen, trying not to make eye contact with anybody else.

'God's curse on you and all Dissenters,' the fat cook flung after her. 'We want none of your canting kind here!'

Eleanor Fairfax scurried through the door, shutting it firmly behind her. She set down the basket and leaned against the wall heaving a sigh of relief. Her shoulders sagged. It had been hard work walking through that wall of hatred. For a moment she stood quietly, deep in her own thoughts. Then she pulled herself together, picked up her basket and began to mount the narrow backstairs that were the servants' access to the upper portion of the house. Elly crept up too, just behind her.

At the top of the stairs was a wooden door. Eleanor opened it and stepped out onto the richly carpeted floor of the upper gallery. Servants hurried to and fro, carrying buckets of water or armfuls of ruffled garments whilst members of the Morton family and their friends strolled up and down the long gallery chatting.

Eleanor Fairfax crossed the long gallery, receiving no sign of recognition from either servants or members of the family. She paused outside one of the rooms, set down her basket. Then she tucked back a few escaping curls of unruly hair, brushed a couple of imaginary specks from her dress, and knocked lightly on the half-open door before pushing it open fully and going into the room. Elly slipped in after her. She remembered this room only too well. It was the one with the four-poster bed. The room where she had felt faint. She looked around. The bed was there, only it had dark red curtains now. And the oak chest was under the window this time, with several long silk gowns carelessly flung across it. Elly pulled a face: the room smelt like the girls' changing rooms at her school after a hockey match.

'Good day, Arbella,' Eleanor said, advancing into the room.

Arbella Morton was sitting on a low wooden stool carefully examining her face in a looking glass held in both hands. She spun round, her eyes lighting up greedily as she saw who had come in.

'Have you brought them?' she exclaimed. Elly noticed she did not even bother to return Eleanor's greeting. Eleanor opened the catch on the basket and drew out a glove and a small cap.

71

'Here,' she said, laying them down on the counterpane. 'I am sorry, but the embroidery took longer than I thought, or you should have had them sooner.'

'Never *mind*!' Arbella impatiently brushed away her apologies. 'At least you have finished them now.' She threw the mirror carelessly down on top of the pile of clothes and danced across the room to the bed. Then she picked up the glove, turning it around, examining it minutely. Eleanor stood watching, her face expressionless. It looked almost as if she couldn't care less what Arbella thought, but Elly knew that her heart was beating furiously, and she was holding her breath, waiting for Arbella's reaction. Arbella turned the glove over and over between her long white fingers.

Why was it so special? Elly wondered.

The lower part of the glove was made out of plain brown leather. The upper portion, however, was made of ruby red velvet, intricately embroidered with golden flowers, apples, and entwining branches. The cap, also made out of red velvet, was richly decorated with gold cord and little gold tassels.

'But this is magnificent work,' Arbella murmured disbelievingly. 'You did it all by yourself?'

Eleanor Fairfax nodded.

'I did not think you could produce such fine work.' Arbella picked up the cap, stroked the embroidery, fiddled with the tiny gold tassels. 'Why, I could not do better, and I was taught by one of the finest seamstresses in Paris.'

Eleanor felt her heart soar. This was worth all the backbreaking hours, her eyes aching as she sewed far into the night, her only light a guttering candle. To have Arbella Morton, with her white skin, fair curls, and all her many accomplishments actually admit that a poor cottage girl had done something better than her!

72

'My embroidery is a gift God has given me,' she said quietly. She stared down at the floor, hoping Arbella wouldn't see her triumphant smile.

'And you shall be well paid for it.' Arbella rose swiftly and went over to the chest by the window. She tossed the dresses and the mirror carelessly aside, picked up a little bag which had been hidden under the pile of clothes and shook out a handful of coins. She placed them in Eleanor's basket.

'This is for your fine sewing. And for keeping my secret safe,' she said. 'The glove and cap are to be my birthday gift to my beloved brother. It is our sixteenth birthday in a few weeks' time, and as soon as I found out that our father had bought a new hawk for him, I was wild to give him something for it. There is to be a great party next week, with feasting and dancing. I shall give it to him then. Of course,' she continued, giving Eleanor a sly look, 'he will never know that you made them. I shall let him think I embroidered them specially for him all by myself. It will make him so happy.'

Eleanor Fairfax walked home. She was content. The money she had earned would buy food for herself and for her imprisoned father. And she would earn more. Her reputation as a seamstress was growing. Several fine ladies had already asked her to make things for them.

The coins jingled in her basket but that was not the only reason for her light step and merry expression. Of course she had suspected who the glove and cap were for— everybody in the village knew that old Hugh Morton had bought a new hawk for his son and was having it secretly trained. Nothing was hidden for long in a small, close community. So as soon as Arbella had summoned her to the house and explained what she wanted, Eleanor had resolved to carry out a secret little plan of her own.

That was why she had embroidered the glove specially, working it to a secret design of her own making. And to her relief, Arbella hadn't noticed a thing. Now, every time Hugh wore the glove, he would be wearing the token of their love for each other. Just like the knights of old wore their ladies' favours, she thought. Eleanor Fairfax reached her cottage. Smiling to herself, she pushed open the door and went inside.

As soon as she was on her own again, Elly began to feel unwell. Her head started throbbing, her whole body felt hot and cold at the same time. Now, she wished she had not left her warm bed. She stumbled through the wood, forcing herself to put one foot in front of the other, pushing herself on. She had to get home before her mum discovered that she was missing.

At last, Elly reached the back gate. Swaying, she unlatched it and lurched up the path towards the cottage. It seemed like a very long way to the back door. Halfway up the path she realized she wasn't going to make it. Her legs felt like lead jellies. Her eyes wouldn't focus properly. Suddenly, her knees buckled and she pitched forwards onto the grass.

Elly lay still. She no longer had the strength or the will-power to go any further. She surrendered to the waves of exhaustion washing over her. Her only hope was that somehow, her mum would find her before nightfall. She shut her eyes and slipped into unconsciousness.

9

'*A whole day!*' Elly sat up in bed. 'You've got to be joking. How did I miss a whole day?'

'You slept through it,' her mum said. 'Don't you remember anything?'

'No.' Elly shook her head. 'What happened?'

'You remember waking up feeling ill?'

'I remember that all right,' Elly grumbled. 'It felt like somebody was drilling a hole in my brain.'

'And I left you in bed while I went to the hospital to check on Aunt Rose—'

'They rang—she was really ill or something, I remember that too,' Elly interrupted.

'When I got back from the hospital, you'd disappeared.'

'I'd *what*?'

'I didn't know what had happened—I was really worried sick. Luckily the woman from next door came round to tell me you were lying outside the back door.'

'I was?'

'And then the police arrived.'

'They *did*?'

'She'd rung them,' her mum sighed. 'I don't think she knows much about teenagers—I'm afraid she thought you'd collapsed after taking drugs.'

'Mum! I would never, ever be that stupid!'

'It caused quite a stir, believe me. A police car with flashing lights—curtains twitching; everybody suddenly finding reasons to be out in their gardens.'

'Not fair,' Elly protested, 'something really exciting happens, and I miss it!'

'Well, console yourself with the thought that you were actually there,' her mum said drily, 'even though you didn't see anything!'

'So then what happened?'

'Oh, this very nice policeman helped me lift you back inside the house. Then I called a doctor. She couldn't find anything wrong with you, said you were probably just a bit dehydrated and you needed to rest.' Her voice broke, 'Oh, Elly, I was really scared when I couldn't find you. What on earth were you doing out in the garden?'

'I don't know.' Elly shook her head, bewildered. She wasn't lying. She really couldn't remember a thing.

'I'm getting quite worried about you.' Her mum's face was anxious as she looked down. 'First you had that funny turn at Morton House. Now this. I'm wondering whether we should have you checked over properly.'

'Mum, I'm fine, honestly,' Elly said quickly. It was true. She felt OK now. As if she'd never been ill. Anyway, the last thing she wanted right now was some doctor fussing over her. 'Hey, it's probably my age, or something,' she said jokingly. 'You're always telling me I'm a pain.' She slid out from under her duvet. 'Look, I can stand up. Watch: I can touch my toes. See, I'm absolutely OK. What's for breakfast?'

'Well, I don't know . . . ' her mum began.

'Toast?' Elly said encouragingly. 'Cereal? A fry-up would be nice. I'm starving.'

'All right, I get the message. All the same, from now on I'm going to keep a close eye on you, just in case. After all, you've never collapsed before, have you? Oh yes . . . ' her mum added, 'what was all that about gloves?'

'Gloves?'

'Gloves. Every now and then you mumbled something about gloves and started laughing.'

'Huh?'

'Well, it was more chuckling: ''He, he, he!'' Like that.'

'Must have been the drugs, I suppose—no, Mum, only kidding, really!'

Gloves—of course! Elly sat on the edge of her bed. Her memory came flooding back. Suddenly, she recalled everything: she'd seen the figures from the past again. She had followed Eleanor Fairfax to Morton House. Witnessed her giving Arbella the glove and the cap. Except this time, it had been different. Instead of *watching* the scene unfold, as if she was an onlooker at a play, she had been part of it. She'd actually felt what Eleanor felt, knew what she was thinking. Just as if she and Eleanor were one person.

Elly shivered. That was really scary!

For the rest of the day, Elly stayed in. She ate, rested, allowed herself to be fussed over. And she drew, filling the pages of her sketchbook with pictures of the past. She felt impelled to get it all down on paper while it was all completely fresh and clear in her mind.

And while she drew, she thought. Her brain trying to create an order and pattern out of the brief snippets that she had seen. She realized that everything was drawing closer and closer to the terrible events leading up to Arbella's murder. That was obvious. But the question remained: who could possibly have killed Arbella? Who could have hidden her body in the chest? Elly was pretty sure it wasn't Hugh, he was devoted to her. And besides, he was such a wimp. As far as Elly could see there were two options. Somebody from the village, as Helen Morton had suggested, or the other option: Eleanor Fairfax had done it.

Eleanor Fairfax. Elly tried to think of a possible motive. She knew Eleanor was in love with Hugh, but to murder his sister—was it possible? What had she to gain by Arbella's death? It would only turn Hugh against her. Logically, everything pointed to the crime being committed by somebody unknown. Unless Eleanor Fairfax had killed both of them. But Elly couldn't get her mind around that one. And there was another thing she was finding hard to take on board: why her? She had no connection with the Morton family or the area. Why was she being drawn slowly and inexorably into the dark mystery that surrounded the twins' deaths?

The next morning, Elly woke to find rain beating against her window. She got up, hoping that it was just a light shower. No such luck. This was rain with the volume turned up. She dressed, swearing under her breath. She wanted her mum to take her into town, treat her to something nice as a got-well present. There were a couple of CDs she had her eye on. She'd dropped a few unsubtle hints. And later on, she'd planned a walk in the woods. Now she faced being stuck indoors for another day. And time was running out. Soon, Aunt Rose would be better. Then they'd have to go home. Elly leaned her cheek against the rain-soaked window pane. How could she go back without finding out who killed Arbella? And how could she return to school, to face Jessica again? She could have wept with frustration.

In the kitchen, she found her mum typing busily on her laptop. 'Just got this report to finish and send,' she said without looking up. 'Mustn't keep clients waiting.'

Elly poured herself some juice. She watched her mum's

fingers moving over the keyboard. Since Elly'd been small, her mum had worked from home. She wrote letters, prepared business documents. She was busy and getting busier as she could work in several languages. Elly was secretly impressed. There were times she found one language hard enough.

'It's raining.'

'Mmmm.'

Elly sighed, propped her chin on her elbows. 'I hate rain.'

'Mmmm.'

'What are we going to do, then?'

'Sorry, I'm going to the hospital this morning.'

'Right.'

'Perhaps we could go somewhere after lunch. Where do you fancy?'

Elly thought. Her face suddenly brightened. 'I know, why don't we go and have another look round Morton House?'

Her mum gave her a look, pinched her lips together. Elly just knew she was dying to make some silly comment about seeing Hugh. Then she nodded. 'All right. If you're sure . . . '

'Yeah. I never got a good look round, did I?' Elly was relieved. Her mum was finally getting the message. Good. She really didn't want another fight.

'Well, you know I always like old houses. I didn't know you did, though.'

'I want to go again, honest.' Elly put some bread in the toaster.

Her mum packed the laptop away. 'I'm sorry this is all a bit boring for you.'

'It's OK.' Elly tried to keep her voice neutral.

'Still, not much longer. Hopefully, we'll soon be back home.'

Elly grunted noncommittally. Little did her mum know, she thought. Right now, home was the very last place she wanted to be.

Morton House did not look its best in the rain. It needed bright sunshine to bring out the colours of the rooftiles, breathe life into the whorls and patterns on the white plasterwork. Seen through a curtain of raindrops, the house appeared dull, the windows grey and lifeless.

Elly shivered. *It's watching me*, she thought. *It doesn't like me*. Suddenly, she knew exactly how Eleanor Fairfax felt as she'd scuttled across the kitchen. She too had to fight the urge to turn around and run back down the front steps. She took a deep breath, told herself not to be stupid. She had wanted to come here. She wasn't going to give up, not now she was getting so close.

Rain had washed away the visitors. Elly and her mum had the place almost to themselves. They crossed the hall, their footsteps echoing loudly, and mounted the grand staircase.

'Lovely carving,' her mum murmured.

Elly stroked the satiny brown wood. *He did a good job, my dad*. She froze. What was she thinking? Her dad worked in Brussels. He hated DIY. He couldn't even knock a nail in straight. Eleanor Fairfax's father had made the staircase.

Get a grip, she told herself severely.

'Shall we go and see that beautiful four-poster bed you liked last time?' her mum asked. She crossed the gallery, went into Arbella's bedroom. Elly followed. Arbella's room—the one with the big oak chest in it. She wanted to check that chest out. But on the threshold she stopped. She could not move. It felt just as if something or somebody was barring her way, preventing her from entering. Elly's heart started to beat like a terrified bird. Her face burned. Fear rose up inside her. In a minute she was sure she was going to scream.

'Elly?' Someone said her name.

Elly spun round. 'Oh, it's you!' she gasped.

'How're you doing?' Hugh Morton asked.

'Good. Yeah, good.'

'You look like you've just seen a ghost.'

Elly faked a smile. 'Er . . . it's nothing. I'm fine,' she said. She moved away from Arbella's room. The spell was broken. *But I did feel something . . . or someone*, she thought.

'Having another look round?' Hugh asked, falling into step.

'Um . . . yeah. We thought we'd come back. See the bits we missed first time.' Elly felt herself blushing. She'd been secretly hoping he'd be here, but she felt embarrassed. She remembered how rude she'd been to him, wondered whether to apologize.

'Gran was really pleased to see you,' Hugh remarked. He appeared to have forgotten their last meeting. 'She told me you'd called round. Thanks for doing that.'

'It was nothing,' Elly replied. 'She's nice. Interesting to talk to.'

'She really liked Flossy,' Hugh went on. They walked together along the gallery. 'Great idea to bring her. I keep telling her she should get a dog. It'd be company for her when I'm at school.'

Elly tried not to let her mind dwell on the subject of school. As if reading her thoughts, Hugh said: 'I suppose you'll be going back soon?'

Elly sighed. 'Suppose so. We can't stay here for ever.'

'Yeah, I have to go back too. My dad's getting stroppy about all the tutoring he's had to pay for. He says I can't afford to miss the end of year exams!'

They reached the far end of the long gallery. Hugh stopped beside a glass case. 'There's something here you'll be interested in,' he said. 'Gran said I should show it to you. Look: one of Hugh Morton's letters to his sister.'

Elly glanced down into the case. There wasn't much of the letter left. Just a few scraps of torn and yellowing paper, the words barely readable.

'Umm . . . it's not very easy to make out, is it?'

'That's why there's a translation underneath,' Hugh said.

'Oh yeah, right. I see it now,' Elly bluffed. She stared at the small piece of card next to the letter. ' "*Dearest and sweetest* . . . " ' she read. ' "*I hope we will soon be* . . . " ' The rest of the sentence was missing . . . ' "*I think of you constantly and remember* . . . " ' Another gap . . . ' "*Until we two shall be together again*".' Dearest and sweetest who? 'There's no name on it,' she said. 'And no signature. Maybe it's from someone else.'

'No, it's definitely from Hugh Morton.' Hugh nodded. 'It's his handwriting. And he always started his letters to his sister "dearest and sweetest".' He looked around, lowering his voice. 'They found the letter on the body. That was how they knew it was Arbella. Nobody else would have carried around one of Hugh's letters.'

'Oh.' Elly looked down again at the yellowing paper with its faded black scrawls. She felt a sudden shiver go down her spine. 'So you actually saw the body then?'

'Afraid not.' Hugh pulled a face. 'It all happened last summer when I was in France, being lectured about my school report. Shame about that.'

'So what happened to it?' Elly asked.

'It's buried in the family vault,' Hugh told her. 'There was a proper funeral service. Gran had a joint headstone made for Arbella and Hugh—even though he isn't there really. Do you want to see it?'

'No way!' Elly shook her head vehemently.

'It isn't spooky,' Hugh insisted. 'It's just quiet and a bit sad. I go there every now and then. It's a good place to sit and think.'

'Ugh!'

'Elly?' her mum's voice broke into her thoughts. 'There you are. Oh, hello, Hugh—how nice to see you again. Elly, I wish you wouldn't go wandering off. I thought you were right behind me. I've just been having this great long conversation with myself!'

'Sorry, Mum,' Elly said. 'I was looking at this letter from Hugh Morton—you know, the twin who vanished.'

'It's my fault, Mrs Laverty.' Hugh smiled winningly. 'I sort of distracted her.'

'Oh well . . . ' Elly watched her mum visibly melt under Hugh's charm. It must run in the family, she thought wryly. 'I suppose that's all right then. Can I see this letter?'

Hugh showed her the torn fragments of paper. They both bent over the case studying it together. Elly wandered off a little way. She had spotted another glass case under the window. She went and leaned on the glass top, peered at the neatly typed label: 'Personal items from the seventeenth and eighteenth centuries'.

Elly stared at the personal items: faded fans with lacy edges and fragile ivory struts, a couple of tiny pill boxes painted with scenes of London, a pair of long fawn stockings. She was just about to turn away, when she saw the glove. It was almost hidden by a lilac parasol.

Elly bent down until her nose was practically touching the glass. She recognized it instantly. The colours had faded over time, and two of the leather fingers had been ripped off, maybe by the hawk, but she would know that glove anywhere.

Eagerly, her eyes followed the intricate patterns of embroidered stems and leaves until she found the initials H and E, lovingly intertwined between the branches. H and E—Hugh and Eleanor. You'd have to have exceedingly sharp eyes to spot them. Eleanor had cunningly disguised the letters, blending them with the flowers and fruit. Elly knew there was also an H and an E on the other side of the glove. HE HE. Instead of HA HA—Hugh and Arbella. It was Eleanor's little triumph, her way of getting back at Arbella Morton for all the slights and put-downs she'd had to endure. For the beautiful clothes that she would never wear and the good food that she'd never taste. It was also her secret message to Hugh Morton, telling him of her love. Had Hugh ever noticed?

You hated her, didn't you . . . ? Elly thought. *She had everything you wanted.* But did that hatred spill over into something more deadly? Elly pictured Eleanor's open, honest face. She was too nice to contemplate anything evil. But she might. Desperation could make you do strange things. Things you'd never normally contemplate doing. As she knew only too well.

10

Elly hadn't meant to take it. She had never taken anything before. She was not a taker—even now, she refused to use the appropriate word.

Looking back, she still couldn't quite believe she'd done it. And so swiftly too. It was a Friday afternoon. They'd had games. She got back first to get changed. The changing room was empty. Jessica Thornton's bag was hanging on a peg by the door. Elly had only meant to peek inside to look for her pen. Then she saw Jessica's sports watch lying on top of her books. Quick as a flash, Elly had grabbed the watch, slipped it up the sleeve of her tracksuit. Then she'd picked up her own bag and left. It only took a second. Nobody saw her.

On the way home, she tried to justify what she'd done. It served Jessica right. She'd stolen Elly's pen so she deserved to lose her watch. Fair exchange. And Jessica was a witch, she'd made Elly's life hell for months. She had it coming. Elly replayed the scene in her mind: the cold, unheated changing room, the row of bags, saw herself going over to Jessica's bag, hesitating. Then the hand sliding into the bag. Supposing, just supposing she had stopped there. Withdrawn her hand. What then? But she could feel the watch bouncing around in her sleeve as she walked. A rhythmic reminder of what she had done.

She reached home. Went up to her room, threw herself onto her bed. She took the watch out of her sleeve, laid it down beside her. The watch seemed to smile smugly up at her: *You know what you are, don't you?* it seemed to be saying. *You know what Jessica will do when she finds out. And she will find out. Too late to put the clock back. You're going to get it now.*

Elly got a hammer from the garage. Then, setting the watch on the floor, she began to pound it into pieces. With fierce joy she brought the hammer down again and again. She felt as if she was not simply destroying Jessica's watch, but Jessica herself, smashing her face into fragments, splintering the bones, crushing her skull into tiny shreds of nothing. It was a terrifyingly wonderful experience. Finally, she swept up all the tiny pieces and binned them. And on Monday, when Jessica complained loudly about losing her precious watch, Elly said nothing. She was secretly exultant. It was a powerful feeling. Much later the full horror of what she had done—what she had wanted to do—came home to her.

So she knew exactly how Eleanor Fairfax felt. But that wasn't proof that she had killed Arbella Morton.

It had been a good afternoon, Elly thought, as they drove the short distance home through the fine rain. She'd got back on track with Hugh. She really liked him. And she'd seen the rest of the house. She wondered how Helen Morton could have lived for so long amongst the rotting wood and mouldy crumbling plaster. It was as if the house itself had died long ago and had been gently decaying over the centuries, like the body in the oak chest.

There had been one embarrassing moment: Hugh offered to take them down to the kitchens—not yet open to the public. Without thinking what century she was in, Elly had tried to take the short cut down the back stairs and had found herself walking straight into an oak panel. She'd managed to laugh it off, mumbling something about needing glasses, but it had shaken her. It was the second time that day she had found herself thinking and behaving like Eleanor Fairfax. Somehow the more she discovered about the past, the more the past was taking over her present.

As soon as they got back, Elly went into the front room and slumped down in front of the TV. She felt totally exhausted. Perhaps she'd overdone it tramping over the house all afternoon. But she had to do it. Time was running out. She knew they couldn't stay here for ever. And she desperately wanted to find out about the murder. She must have dozed off in front of the screen; the next thing she knew was her mum bringing in a tray with a bowl of soup and some toast.

'You look all in,' she said, setting the tray down next to Elly. 'Hot bath and an early night?' Elly stirred the soup round with her spoon and nodded, too tired to protest that she never went to bed before eleven.

'I'll go and run the bath for you now.'

Elly finished her food. She decided to take a book upstairs, just in case sleep eluded her. She selected one from Aunt Rose's collection and carried it up to her room. She need not have worried, almost as soon as she'd got into bed, she felt her eyelids closing.

It was dark when she awoke, although a glance at her watch told her that it was only ten-thirty. Through her open door, Elly heard her mum downstairs talking to somebody. She got out of bed and crept onto the landing. Her mum was on the phone. Elly sat herself down on the top step, listening in the unlit gloom.

'Yes . . . I think so,' she heard her mum say. 'Well, it's hard to tell, you know what hospitals are like, they never give you the whole picture. Yes . . . soon, I hope. Can't stay here much longer, I've got a business to run . . . ' There was a pause. Then: 'No . . . no, I haven't told her yet.' Another pause. A sigh. 'Well, there simply hasn't

87

been the right moment. You can't just announce something like that, can you?' Elly felt her heart lurch uncomfortably. It must be her dad on the other end of the phone. And she guessed what her parents were talking about. 'Yes, of course I'm going to tell her. We agreed that, didn't we? It's just that I'll have to pick my moment . . .' More silence. 'Oh, I know that's how you'd do it. And I'd be left to pick up the pieces, wouldn't I. No, I don't want to upset her. Yes, of course she's going to be upset— what did you think, she's just going to accept it? Yes, I'll let you know. Soon. Yes. Right. Bye.' There was the sound of the phone being put down. Her mum going into the kitchen, filling the kettle.

Elly crept back to her room and got into bed once more. She pulled the duvet over her head, shutting the world out. Hot tears trickled down her cheek and soaked into her pillow. She felt the book slipping off the bed onto the floor. Dimly she was aware that a small piece of cardboard had fluttered out, but she was far too miserable to bother investigating it.

11

Elly awoke next morning with a heavy heart and to the sound of a strange, rhythmical thumping noise accompanied by an eerie whine. She sat up, eyes wide-open. Then relaxed. It was only Flossy, head-butting her bedroom door, demanding to be taken out. Elly glanced at her watch: ten past seven.

'Oh no!' she moaned, burying her face under the pillow.

'It's your turn,' her mum called out sleepily from her room. 'I've walked her for the last few mornings so I'm due a lie-in!'

Cursing, Elly got up, reached for her jeans and a sweatshirt. Leaving her mum to enjoy her lie-in, she went down to the silent kitchen. Flossy was already sitting on the mat in the scullery, treating the back door to a look that could blister paintwork and melt wood.

So now she knew the truth about her parents, Elly thought. They were splitting up. Her mum was only waiting for the right moment to tell her. Well, how kind, she thought grimly. She wondered when the 'right moment' would arrive. Today? Tomorrow? After it had happened? Maybe she'd create the right moment herself and confront her mum directly. Suddenly, Elly realized how much she'd been hoping this wouldn't happen. Time for a reality check. She had to put her hopes on a high shelf, out of mind. Pretend she never had them in the first place.

She decided to go down the lane and through the fields.

89

Her mum said it was Flossy's favourite walk and that they passed a field of miniature Shetland ponies on the way. Elly slipped some bread and a few carrots into a plastic carrier and got the spaniel's lead from the scullery. One thing about this holiday, she thought to herself, she was going to end up a lot fitter than she'd ever been before. She'd walked miles.

The path across the fields was completely deserted. Elly remembered her mum saying this path was once an old drover's road, used to drive sheep and cattle to the local market and then on to London. It must have been a long journey, she thought, as they approached the field with the ponies. Elly fed them the titbits she had brought, enjoying their warm smell and the feel of their tickly breath on her hand. Then she crossed over the wooden stile that led to a common.

She slipped the lead and let Flossy run about exploring. A few minutes, dog, Elly thought. She had two tricky situations to deal with today: she wanted to confront her mum, get to the truth whilst she still felt brave enough; and she'd also decided the time had come to talk to Hugh. He ought to know what was happening. Some of it, anyway. After all, they were his ancestors. Elly pulled a face. She didn't want Hugh to think she was mad. She'd have to work out what she was going to say carefully. She glanced at her watch and whistled to the spaniel before turning round to retrace her steps.

Elly had just reached the crest of the hill, almost in sight of the row of cottages, when she saw a little procession in the distance. At first, it wasn't a procession at all, merely a moving cloud of dust, too far away for her to make it out clearly, but as it drew nearer Elly saw a group of people on horseback and a covered wagon. She knew who the people were. Almost unbidden, as if she had known them all her life, the names slipped into her mind.

At the head of the procession, riding the black mare that Arbella had so coveted was Hugh Morton, head of the Morton family. He sat very upright in his saddle, looking neither to left nor right. On his head he wore a long curled wig under a fine wide-brimmed black hat gaily decorated with ostrich-plumes and he carried his head erect, his shrewd blue eyes staring at the road ahead, his mouth set and tight under his thin, fair moustache.

Behind him rode his steward Samuel Leyburn, carrying Anne Morton, riding pillion on the same horse, her yellow silk dress billowing around her in the warm breeze. She too, was staring in front of her, blue eyes cold and hard as steel, her nose in the air, as if she had just smelt something rotten. Behind them came John and Robert Morton, the two elder sons, also on fine horses, then Ned, another servant, with Arbella, in a sky-blue gown, riding pillion behind him. She was followed closely by the wagon, from which Elly could hear the sounds of children quarrelling and a baby wailing fretfully. Then more servants and finally six pack horses, laden down with boxes and bundles.

'Well, there they go. Off to London to enjoy themselves. A fine sight for a spring morning, is it not?'

Elly jumped. She had not heard the man come up behind her and yet suddenly, there he was at her shoulder, a lean, tall grey-haired man, his face lined and pale in an unhealthy way suggestive of too much confinement indoors and not enough good food. His plain, coarse brown workman's clothes smelt of musty sawdust and his hands were rough and calloused. Elly had never seen him before in her life, but she knew who he was.

'Aye, father,' she answered automatically. Now she knew why the riders were keeping their eyes so firmly fixed upon the road. They were pretending not to see him. Or rather, not to see them both. Suddenly, Elly realized that she must have become Eleanor Fairfax. It was a strange feeling, rather like putting on somebody else's clothes.

'Look well at their faces, daughter,' the man went on, deliberately raising his voice as the procession passed within a few feet of where they were standing. 'Look at their proud expressions. They don't see us. Just because the Mortons have costly clothes and houses and money, they think they are better than us poor hard-working country folk, but I promise you, in the eyes of God, they are not. Yes, Hugh Morton,' the man was almost shouting now, 'the Lord knows you. You may be rich, but your charity is as cold as your heart. All that time in prison, and you never once sent me any relief, in spite of the work I have done for you and your fine house.'

'Father!' Eleanor felt her face going red with shame and embarrassment.

'A man should quake with awe before his God!' Matthew Fairfax shouted, almost beside himself with rage, little rivulets of spit running down his chin. 'He should not ride abroad on a fine horse for all the world as if he owned the world. I tell you, Hugh Morton, your pride will be your downfall one day, mark what I say!'

His words echoed eerily in the early morning silence. The procession passed them by.

'Huh!' Matthew Fairfax spat contemptuously. 'Vile Protestants! We are well rid of them and their canting ways.'

'Father, you did not have to be so . . . '

'I did not see young Hugh with them.'

'No, he has already gone to London,' Eleanor began and then stopped, the colour flooding to her face.

'So . . . ' Matthew Fairfax's eyes narrowed. 'Your face betrays you. It is true what I have heard then. About you and he meeting each other secretly, whilst I was in prison.' He gripped her arm tightly and shook her. 'Listen to me, daughter. Whatever thoughts you may have of that weak-minded pretty boy, put them out of your head right now. He is a Morton. He is just like the rest of them.'

'But, father—'

'No more! Tomorrow, I shall write to your brother in Amwell to come for you and that will be the end of this folly! Do you understand me?'

Mutely, Eleanor nodded, tears starting to her eyes. She felt as if somebody had set a great leaden weight upon her chest and her heart was cracking open.

'Come now,' Matthew Fairfax spoke more kindly, 'dry your eyes, daughter, for I promise you, he is not worth the smallest tear. Believe me, he will soon forget about you once he gets to London. Let us return to the house. *We* have an honest day's work ahead of us both.'

He took her arm and drew her away. For a moment, Elly felt the touch of his hand, then the sensation faded. The man vanished and she found herself alone once again, with Flossy running round her in circles, barking madly.

Elly turned and stared along the path. She almost expected to see the Morton family and their servants disappearing into the distance, but there was nothing. Just the wide blue sky and a few skylarks rising from the fields. For a while, she stood waiting to see if anything else was about to materialize, then, whistling to Flossy, she turned round and set off home.

That had been really weird, Elly thought, re-tracing her steps. For a while, she had actually been two people at the same time. Two people, separated by over three hundred years. It was like one of those dreams, she thought, where everything seems so real that you believe in it completely, whilst at the back of your mind you know that all the time it is only a dream.

So now she had seen the whole Morton family.

Matthew Fairfax was right. They were proud. That summed them up exactly. They looked just like the portraits that she'd seen at the house. Stiff, stony-faced, and unsmiling. Elly had thought that was the way they painted people in the seventeenth century. Now she knew better. It also explained the atmosphere in the house. Pride hung about it like a cold fog, as if the spirits of the Mortons still walked the dark galleries, their stuck-up noses in the air.

Elly remembered too the terrible words Matthew Fairfax had flung at the departing family. Words that had flown after them like vengeful black crows. Matthew Fairfax did not know that his prophecy would come true. Something would happen that would bring the proud Mortons down. She knew however, with the wisdom of hindsight, that the family was travelling on the road of death: their death from plague. They were all going to perish in London, except for Hugh and Arbella, who would somehow be smuggled out of the city. And then? And then Elly realized with a stab of fear, history would repeat itself. The terrible events that ended with Arbella's body being found in the chest, were about to happen all over again. With one difference: this time, she was going to be involved in it. Elly opened the back door, went into the kitchen. Maybe this wasn't like a dream after all. Maybe it was rapidly becoming a nightmare.

There was a note on the kitchen table. It said: *Gone to shops, then hospital. Back later*. Then in large letters: TIDY UP YOUR ROOM!! Elly looked at her watch. She'd been out longer than she'd thought. Damn. She'd psyched herself up to confront her mum. Discover the truth about what was going on with her dad. Now she'd have to find another time. Work herself up to it again. She fed the dog, made herself some peanut butter toast. She'd thought it was going to be OK here. But it was turning out the same as at home: everything was getting complicated. Hard to stand back and be objective. She felt confused, unsure of herself.

When she'd finished her late breakfast, Elly got the Hoover and went upstairs. There was no getting away from it, her bedroom was a tip. There was stuff everywhere, clothes, drawing pencils, empty Coke cans, and crisp packets. It was beginning to look exactly like her bedroom back home. She began picking things up and stuffing them in drawers or in the black plastic bag her mum had rather pointedly left in the middle of the room.

Ten minutes later, she stood back to admire the effect. It looked pretty good, she thought, just so long as her mum didn't actually open any of the drawers, or look in the wardrobe. She ran the Hoover over the floor for a second or so. It would have to do. She had done enough tidying. Elly sat down on the bed, the silence, oppressive, pressing in on her. Suddenly, she felt she couldn't stay in Aunt Rose's claustrophobic little house on her own any longer. She had to get out before the walls closed in and smothered her. She bent down, reached for her trainers, which she'd kicked off earlier. It was then she noticed an oblong piece of card. Curious, Elly picked it up, turned it over.

On the other side of the card was a small black-and-white photograph. A smiling woman in a flowered sundress and a little girl aged maybe three or four, in a bathing costume. They were in a garden. The woman was standing up, the girl sitting at her feet, holding a toy dog. Amazed, Elly stared down at the tiny photo. Where had it come from? Then she remembered something falling out of the book she'd borrowed. It must have been this photo. She recognized the woman at once. *It's Mum*, she thought—she'd seen photos of her mum when she was a young woman. And the little girl must be herself. How weird. Why on earth did Aunt Rose have a photo of her and Mum?

Elly examined the photo again closely. She frowned. Could it really be a photo of her and Mum? They didn't have any black-and-white photos at home, she thought, her dad always took colour pictures. She stared at the photo again. There was definitely a family resemblance though. The young woman looked just like her mum. Spitting image. But the little girl—a closer examination showed that she lacked Elly's pinch-pointed face, dark apple-seed eyes. Her wild halo of black frizzy hair. Strange though. If the two people weren't her and Mum, then who were they? Elly ran out onto the landing.

'Mum?' she called down hopefully. 'Are you there? Come and see what I've found.'

There was no answer. Elly slipped the photo carefully into the back pocket of her jeans. She would have to find out about it later. She went downstairs. The dog looked up at her hopefully. Elly found the lead. 'Come on then!' she said. 'Let's get out of here.'

12

Helen Morton was planting pansies in the front garden. She was wearing a battered old straw hat and a pair of baggy workmen's dungarees. She straightened up as Elly and the dog walked by, wiping her earthy hands on her dungarees.

'Elly! Come on in.' She opened the gate.

Flossy greeted her ecstatically. Elly slipped off the lead. The spaniel went straight over to investigate the newly planted flowerbed.

'How nice to see you again,' Helen Morton smiled. 'And with my favourite dog too. What a treat.'

'We were just on a walk,' Elly lied. She had deliberately chosen the route that led to the gatehouse. She had also deliberately gone by the road rather than through the woods. To avoid the Mortons. She didn't want to be distracted. She had a lot of hard thinking to do on the way.

'Can you stop for a bit? I'm sure Hugh will be delighted to see you. He's doing some schoolwork inside.'

Elly had every intention of stopping. She'd reached a decision: she was fed up with being part of someone else's gruesome past. Time to share the nightmare. It was Hugh's family, he could deal with it.

'I'll go and tell him you're here.'

Of course, Hugh wouldn't believe her. Tough. She had proof. Things she knew about the Mortons that he didn't. Not that she was worried whether he believed her or not. Telling might just stop the past dragging her back. So it was worth a try. She waited for Hugh, trying not to notice the earth and stones flying up from the far end of the garden where the dog was digging holes.

'Hugh says to come straight in.' Helen Morton came back out into the garden.

Hugh was sitting at a table in the back room, working on a maths problem. 'Five minutes and I'm done,' he said. Elly perched on the narrow window seat. She could just see the red tiled roof and twisty chimneys of Morton House sticking up above the trees.

'Here, you might like to borrow these.' Hugh passed her his CD player and headphones. Elly listened to the music. It wasn't a band she'd heard before, but it was good.

Finally Hugh slapped the book shut. 'OK?' he mouthed.

Elly slipped off the headphones. 'Good band,' she said, handing them back.

'You liked it?'

'Yeah. I've never heard them before.'

'No, you wouldn't have. They're from my school.'

'Oh really? What's their name?'

'Anal Fissure.'

'Eww . . . good name.'

'I thought of it.'

'Do you play in the band?' Elly was impressed.

'Yeah—I'm the bass guitarist,' Hugh said. 'Which is another reason why I have to get back. We've got a gig coming up and I need to practise with them.'

Elly had not planned for this. 'So you're going back to school soon?' she asked.

'Probably in a couple of days,' Hugh said.

'Oh.' Elly tried to keep her voice neutral. She did a swift mental recheck. Hesitated, but only for a fraction of a second. She'd made her decision on the way over. There was too much going on in her life. She had to offload some of it.

'So, how are you doing?' Hugh said.

'Yeah, good.' Elly was desperately thinking of a way of getting into what she really wanted to say. It wasn't so easy.

'Your aunt still in hospital?'

Elly nodded. 'Mmm.' There was a silence. She fiddled with the bone acorn on the window blind. Hugh watched her.

'You look like you've got something on your mind,' he observed.

'Yeah, I have,' Elly said. 'And it's a bit difficult to say it.' She dropped the acorn, paused. 'Look. Remember that drawing I did, the one of Arbella Morton—the one you said looked exactly like her . . . '

'Yes . . . what about it?'

'Well,' Elly went on, 'see, I didn't copy one of the paintings in the house, like I said.'

'No? So it was an accidental likeness then?'

Elly took a deep breath. Here goes nothing, she thought. 'Not exactly,' she said slowly. 'I actually saw her, Arbella Morton, I mean. That was how I was able to draw her so well.'

Hugh frowned. 'Sorry, don't get it. You *saw* her—what do you mean? Where did you see her?'

Elly looked him full in the face. 'I saw her in the wood. Soon after we'd arrived. And I saw Hugh Morton too. Remember, I told you I thought they were actors. Only they weren't.'

'*What!*'

'Look,' Elly said quietly, 'can you do me a big favour? Can you just listen and not say anything. This is quite complicated to explain and I need to get it right.'

Sunlight poured in through the window. Outside in the garden, Helen Morton's voice could be heard. She was talking to Flossy. The silence in the room was deafening. Hugh sat motionless, staring at the table, flicking the cover of his textbook back and forth.

'Say something,' Elly said.

'What do you want me to say?'

'I don't know. Anything.'

Hugh slowly shook his head.

'I'm not mad,' Elly said steadily. 'And I didn't imagine it.'

'No,' Hugh lifted his head and looked at her. 'I know you're not mad.'

'So?'

'So I'm just finding all this a bit hard to get my head around.'

'Do you believe me?'

'Sort of. It's just that it seems so unlikely. I mean, why you and not me? After all, it is my family.'

'I know,' Elly sighed. 'I don't understand why me either.'

'And another thing, why now, after all this time?'

'I think perhaps it's because they found the body,' Elly said slowly. 'It might have released things from the past. Maybe Arbella's spirit.' She'd deliberately chosen the word 'spirit'. Hugh didn't believe in ghosts. So he'd said.

There was another long pause. 'Do you think that could be why?' Elly ventured, cautiously.

'Yeah.' Hugh nodded. 'I guess that could be it. It's logical. And now you think she's trying to tell us who killed her.'

'Something like that.'

'Right.' Hugh's eyes suddenly gleamed. 'Excellent.'

'Not really. Well, not if you're me. It's a bit scary.'

'Well, you're not on your own any more, are you?' Hugh said, getting up.

'No . . . ' Elly said cautiously. 'So, now what?'

Hugh thought for a couple of seconds. 'OK, here's the plan. We'll check out the house—I'd like to see that glove for myself. Then, we'll check out the woods. You show me exactly where you saw them.'

'OK. Then what?'

'Then, well . . . ' he shrugged.

'It doesn't happen to order,' Elly told him. 'We might not see them.'

'OK, I accept that,' Hugh said. 'But we might. It's definitely worth a try.'

Elly stood up. 'I'd better get the dog, then.'

Hugh piled up his books on the table. 'What about Gran?' he asked. 'Shall I tell her?'

Elly sighed. Making plans, telling other people—things were already getting complicated. What a surprise! Sometimes she wished she could keep her mouth shut. 'Does she have to know?' she said. Hugh gave her an injured look. 'OK, tell her,' Elly said. 'But not now. Later, when I've gone. I don't expect she'll believe you, anyway,' she muttered under her breath.

As they reached the front door, Hugh caught her by the elbow. 'Listen,' he said urgently. 'From now on, don't go anywhere on your own. If anything's going to happen to you, I want to be there as well. Deal?'

'Deal,' Elly agreed. She'd have agreed to almost anything: Hugh believed her. She hadn't thought it would be this easy.

Out in the garden, Flossy was lolling on the grass panting, her muzzle and paws covered in earth, whilst Helen Morton sat back on her heels, ruefully surveying her flowerbed. It looked as if it had been attacked by giant moles.

'Oh no!' Elly exclaimed. 'You bad dog! Look at the mess you've made.'

'We'll take her off your hands now, Gran,' Hugh said.

Helen Morton sighed. 'Maybe that might be a good idea,' she nodded. 'Somehow, I don't think this dog will ever be a good gardener.'

Elly bent down and clipped Flossy's lead onto her collar. 'Come on, you disgusting scut of a dog,' she said sternly. 'Walkies.'

They set off up the path that led to Morton House. It was a fine morning; the car park was full of coaches and mini buses. Visitors were everywhere. Hugh and Elly stood outside on the steps, behind a group of tourists waiting to go in.

'We could go round the back,' Hugh suggested. 'Avoid the queue.'

But Elly could not move. The feeling of fear was so strong that she knew she'd never be able to get through the door. Eleanor's fear. She shivered. She had not told Hugh about her and Eleanor. She was not sure he'd believe that part of the story.

'You go,' she said quietly. 'I'll stay out here.'

Hugh looked at her, frowning. 'Why?'

'I've got to mind the dog.'

'I could find somebody to look after her.'

'No, it's not fair. She'll only play up. I'm supposed to be in charge of her.'

'Well, if you're sure . . . ' Hugh hesitated.

'Sure. You're not going to be long are you?'

'No. Look, you won't go anywhere on your own?'

'I'll sit on that bench over there. Go on. I won't move, promise.'

'All right then. See you in five.'

Hugh turned, walked up the front steps and disappeared into the house.

Elly slumped down on the seat, letting the lead out so that the spaniel could go off a little way and sniff around. She glanced at her watch. Five minutes? Unlikely. Hugh could be any time. He would have to stop and chat to the house guides. They all seemed to know him. He might be ages. And all she could do was wait.

She knew this feeling of dread was linked directly to Eleanor Fairfax. The more she became Eleanor, the more scared she felt. Now, it was taking all her strength just to keep sitting on the bench. Waves of panic were rising up inside. She started breathing quickly, desperately wanting to run away. Elly shut her eyes, gripped the edge of the seat tight, fighting for control. She prayed Hugh would be back soon. She wasn't sure she could hang on much longer.

Meanwhile, a party of old people suddenly appeared round the side of the house, coming back from visiting the gardens. Some were in wheelchairs, pushed by helpers; a few walked with frames or sticks. Elly hastily reeled in Flossy, in case she got her lead tangled up with them.

The party made its way slowly past her bench, a few of the old ladies nodding at her and smiling at Flossy. Elly wasn't really paying them much attention, so it was some time before she realized that she was being spoken to. Or rather, being shouted at very crossly, in a cracked old voice.

'Lisbeth Cooper! Lisbeth Cooper! What are you doing here?'

Startled, Elly looked up. An old man in a wheelchair had stopped right beside her. He was leaning across and peering at her curiously.

'I'm sorry?'

'You bin on yer holidays then?' the old man said. 'I ain't seen yer round for ages. Got a nice tan, haven't you?'

The young nurse pushing the wheelchair made 'Don't-mind-him-he's-OK-really' faces over the top of the old man's bald head. 'Now, come along, Mr Baxter,' she coaxed soothingly. 'We don't want to miss our bus, do we?' She caught hold of the chair's handles and was just about to trundle the old man off, when Elly cried, 'No, wait!' She suddenly remembered that her mum's single name was Elisabeth Cooper. And she'd been brought up round here. Coincidence? Elly decided to try and find out. The nurse frowned, but brought the wheelchair back to where she was sitting.

'Please don't keep him chatting too long,' she said primly. 'We have had a very long morning.'

The old man pulled a horrible gurning face at her, but fortunately only Elly saw it. She grinned at him and he winked back, conspiratorially.

'Have you had a nice time?' Elly asked politely, but the old man rudely ignored her question completely. Instead, he pointed a disgusting, bent, nicotine-stained finger down at Flossy, who was investigating the wheels of his chair.

'That your dog then, Lisbeth?'

'No, she belongs to somebody else,' Elly told him.

The old man grunted. 'Thought so. Didn't think your dad would let you have a dog. Mean old bugger that Arthur Cooper!'

'Mr Baxter, please,' the nurse hissed. 'There is no need to use bad language in front of the girl.'

'Mean old bugger I said!' the old man repeated, deliberately raising his voice. 'And a mean old bugger he was an' all. You din't know him.'

The nurse pursed her lips disapprovingly. 'Right then,' she sniffed. 'If you are going to be awkward, we had better go.'

'No, hang on a minute!' Elly had an idea. The photograph, the one she had picked up from under her bed. Suppose she had got it all wrong. Maybe it was not a picture of her and her mum, like she had first thought, but a picture of her mum and *her* mother. One generation back. That made more sense. It would fit with the style of clothes the woman in the picture was wearing. It would explain why the photo was in black and white instead of colour. With a feeling of growing excitement, Elly fished the photograph out of her pocket and showed it to the old man.

'Please, do you recognize these people?' she asked. She held her breath as she waited for his reply.

The old man took the photo, squinted down at it. His wrinkled face broke into a broad gummy grin of pleasure, 'Of course I do,' he crooned. 'That's Rose Cooper. And that little girl's you, Lisbeth, innit? Must have been taken in your garden. You had a nice garden.'

Elly nodded, scarcely able to believe what she was hearing. Rose Cooper and Aunt Rose. There wouldn't be two members of the family with an identical name. They must be the same person. Suddenly Elly felt as if she couldn't breathe. Her heart was beating so fast. She felt as if she was on the edge of making a discovery that was going to change her life for ever.

'So you knew my . . . *mother*?' she whispered, hoping that the old man still thought she was Elisabeth Cooper.

The old man gave a wheezy chuckle. ''Course I knew her,' he croaked. 'We grew up together. Mind, she wasn't called Cooper in them days, but I remember her all right. Prettiest girl in the village.'

Elly stared at the old man. She was stunned. She felt as if all the breath had been knocked out of her.

'You feeling all right?' the old man leaned forward in his chair. 'You don't look too clever.'

'I'm fine,' Elly heard herself say. It was probably the biggest lie she'd ever told in her whole life.

'Now, I'm really going to have to take you back to the bus, Mr Baxter,' the nurse interrupted. 'The others will all be waiting to go home.'

'Can I walk with you?' Elly asked.

'Yer, you come along and welcome,' the old man wheezed. 'Always had an eye for a pretty girl, I did,' and he chuckled fruitily.

Elly got up and walked alongside the wheelchair, keeping Flossy firmly on her other side, so that the spaniel didn't get caught up in the wheels. They rounded the corner of the house and made their way across the gravel drive to the car park, where the rest of the group was being loaded slowly into a large mini-bus with the words Amwell Social Services painted on the side.

Amwell—the village where Aunt Rose had supposedly moved from. It was making more and more sense. 'Nice bus, ain't it?' Mr Baxter remarked. 'Very comfortable inside.'

The nurse pushed the wheelchair up to the rear of the bus, where there was a ramp already lowered and waiting. 'Say goodbye now, Mr Baxter,' she commanded.

'No, wait, one more question,' Elly cried, clinging on to one of the metal arms of the chair. 'Have you seen Rose Cooper lately?'

The old man frowned and sucked in his breath. 'Nope,' he said. 'I never did see her much after she married Arthur. He didn't like anyone talking to her. Specially people like me.' He dug Elly playfully in the ribs with a sharp bony elbow. 'I'm yer original dirty old man, I am. I did hear how Rose moved away after Arthur passed on. Couldn't bear to stay in the village. Mind you, I didn't see much of her anyway, not after all that business . . . well, I don't have to tell you about it, do I. God bless her, I say. She was a lovely girl, was Rose. I courted her for years, you know. She should have married me, not him. I'd have let her have a little dog. We'd have been happy together.' The rest of the sentence was lost in a fit of coughing and choking so severe that tears streamed down the old man's leathery cheeks.

'Right, Mr Baxter,' the nurse said briskly. 'That is quite enough. You're going to make yourself ill, if you carry on like this. On the bus now.' She pushed the chair purposefully onto the ramp. The old man waved a thin veiny hand as the hoist lifted him up into the bus. Elly waved back and watched as a couple of helpers wheeled him to his seat and fastened him in securely. She stood watching until the bus had passed out of sight down the drive.

As soon as the bus had gone, Elly set off home at a run. Her head was in a whirl. Now she knew why the hospital had rung them. Why her mum had been prepared to drop everything to come here. Aunt Rose was not some vague relative her mum had known from her childhood, she was her mother! It all fell into place. A door had suddenly been unlocked. She'd been allowed to see inside a room that she'd never entered before. So many thoughts and emotions whirled around Elly's head. One, however, was uppermost: she had been told lies. All her life, her mum and dad had lied to her. Deliberately. They had kept her from knowing her grandparents. They had even told her that her grandparents had died. Lies, every word of it. But it hadn't worked. She had found out who Aunt Rose really was. At last she reached the top of Aunt Rose's lane. Flossy, panting and whining, dragged along behind her. In the distance, Elly saw her mother's car parked outside the cottage. Good. It was time for the truth. The whole truth! She rushed up the front path, slamming the gate behind her.

13

Elly stormed into the house. Flossy, picking up her mood, pranced and barked around her legs.

'Mum? Where are you?'

'In the kitchen.'

Almost kicking the spaniel aside, Elly flew down the narrow hallway. Hot anger flamed inside her.

'There you both are.' Elly's mum looked up calmly from her laptop. 'I was about to send out a search party. Lunch has been ready for ages.' She seemed not to notice Elly's furious face. 'Have you been seeing Hugh?'

The bitter accusing words died on Elly's lips. Groaning, she threw herself into a chair and stared down at her feet. Stupid, stupid!! She'd completely forgotten Hugh. She'd run off and left him. What would he think? That she'd been caught up in the past? Possibly. That she'd broken her promise to him? Almost certainly. Elly screwed up her face in frustration. Swore under her breath. Why did everything have to be so complicated?

'Elly? I was speaking to you.'

Elly lifted her head, stared at her mum. It was funny, she thought, you could live with a person, think you knew them really well. Then something happened, and you realized that you didn't know them at all. Now, as she looked at her mum, Elly felt suddenly as if she was sitting opposite a total stranger.

'Elly? I got you a cheese and pineapple pizza for your lunch. Would you like me to re-heat it? Elly? What is it? Why are you looking at me like that?'

Slowly and carefully, Elly pulled the photograph out of her pocket and laid it down, picture side up, on the table. She waited, saying nothing. Her mum put out a hand, drew the photo towards her and picked it up. There was a long silence.

'Where did you find this?'

'It fell out of a book I borrowed,' Elly said. 'I thought it was a picture of you and me. But it isn't, is it? It's you and your mother.'

Her mum cradled the tiny photograph in one hand, stared down at it, a look of total amazement on her face.

'You've always told me your mother is dead,' Elly went on. 'But she isn't, is she? She's still alive.'

'How do you know?' Her mum still stared at the photo. Not meeting Elly's eye.

'I met somebody today, an old man, who remembered her from when she was young.' Elly's voice was starting to shake as her anger flamed up. 'He grew up with her in Amwell. He told me that he used to go out with her before she married and became Rose Cooper. That's when I realized who she was. Aunt Rose. Only she isn't an aunt, is she? She is your mother.'

Elly's mum sat very still, not saying anything.

'You lied, Mum,' Elly cried. 'All that time, you lied. And Dad too. You always tell me not to lie but you lied.'

Elly's mum winced, pursed her lips as though she'd tasted something sour.

'Why, Mum?' Elly persisted. 'Whatever happened, it couldn't have been that bad.'

Her mum put the photo down. Looked across the table at Elly. 'Couldn't it?' she said bitterly. She switched off the laptop. 'Yes, OK, Elly, I lied to you. But not for the reasons you think. I lied because there was no point telling you the truth. Because it would have hurt too many people.'

'And now?'

'And now, I suppose, I'll have to tell you. Won't I.'

'Amwell was a small village back then.' Elly's mum folded her arms, rested her elbows on the table. 'Everyone knew everybody else. There were a couple of shops. One bus twice a day. A man came round every Friday in a van selling fruit and vegetables.' She paused. 'It was like living in another world. You walked everywhere, or got the bus into town. Neighbours helped each other, looked out for each other.'

'Sounds OK.'

'It was a good place to grow up in—you could ride a bike anywhere, play in the fields safely. Only, as you got older, there was less and less to do. No cinema, no youth club. Nothing. The biggest thrill was hanging round the bus shelter. The nearest big town was miles away. And the buses didn't run late on a Saturday.'

'So not so good then.'

'People always go on about living in the countryside,' her mum said thoughtfully. 'But they don't know what it can be like. Especially when you're young. I hated it. It was like being in a small glass box. Everybody could see in. You couldn't do anything. No privacy. I couldn't wait to leave. There was a world out there and I wanted to explore it.'

'So?' Elly was leaning forward, chin propped on hands, her eyes fixed on her mum's face. This was the first time they'd talked properly for ages. No fighting. Like two equals.

'I wanted to go to college. Secretarial and business. I thought I'd get away from the village, make something of my life. I had it all planned out. Two years at college, travel for a bit. America, I thought. Then a well-paid job somewhere.'

'Sounds great.'

'Yes. I thought so. But my parents didn't want me to leave.' She paused. Sighed. 'Especially my father . . . '

'*Mean old bugger . . . '* Mr Baxter's words came back to Elly.

'He wanted me to stay at home, get a job locally. Pay my way. He told me I owed it to him and my mum. It was my duty, he said. It was a word he used a lot. My duty to stay and help them out.'

'But that's unfair,' Elly protested.

'Yes. It was. He was a bully—sounds terrible to say that about your own father, doesn't it? But he was. He bullied my mother terribly and he bullied me. He told me I had to forget my big dreams, not try to rise above my station— that was another one of his favourite phrases. And then the rows started. On and on, day after day. He'd shout and rave at me. Call me selfish and ungrateful and I'd shout back. Tell him he had no right to stop me having a future. It was terrible. And my poor mother tried to keep the peace between us.'

Elly thought of the rows her parents had. They were nothing compared to this. 'It must have been tough,' she said sympathetically.

Elly's mum nodded. 'It was. Anyway, in the end we reached a sort of compromise. I left school at sixteen, got a job locally. Then as soon as I was eighteen, I applied to college—one a long way from home.'

'Bet your dad didn't like that.'

'He didn't. Not at all. But he couldn't stop me. I was eighteen. I could do what I liked. But I felt sorry for my mum when I left. I knew things would be hard for her. I used to phone her, during the day when I knew he was at work. And then, in my last year at college, I met your dad. And all hell broke loose.

'You always think people will accept things. Especially

111

when you're young. But there was no way my father was ever going to accept him. The first time I brought him home to meet them was the last time I ever set foot in that house. My father went at us both hammer and tongs. Swearing and shouting at the top of his voice. The whole neighbourhood must have heard every word. In the end he more or less threw us out of the house. It was terrible.'

'*I didn't see much of her after all that business . . .*'

'We sent them an invitation to the wedding, though I knew they wouldn't come. They didn't even reply. But the day before we got married, my mum turned up at the flat we'd rented. I never knew what excuse she must have made to my father to leave the house for a whole day and go somewhere all on her own—it was unheard of! Anyway, there she was.'

'So what did she say?' Elly asked.

'Oh, not much. It was a very sad meeting. She could only stop for a little while—she had to get back before my dad returned from work. She was so scared of him. Always had been. I think I know why, now. It was because he used to hit her.'

'God, that's evil!'

'She often had odd bruises on her face. She used to tell me she'd bumped herself against things. I believed it. Maybe I wanted to. Anyway, she said she wanted to see me again, just one more time. She explained that she couldn't see me any more, because of my father, and I told her I wouldn't see her any more, for the same reason and that was the last time I did see her, until the phone call from the hospital.'

'Oh, Mum, that is so sad,' Elly said.

'I wanted to contact her, every now and then, when something important happened, like moving house, or when you were born, but your dad always said no. He said they'd made their bed and they must lie on it. I suppose he felt hurt too. And very angry. My father had said terrible things. That was why we told you they'd died—it made things easier. But I always grieved for my mum. She didn't deserve what happened.'

'Poor Aunt Rose.' Elly said the name softly.

'I named you after her.'

'*Elrose*,' Elly said wonderingly. 'I always wondered where you'd got that name from.'

'There's something else, too,' Mrs Laverty said. 'A year after we got married, she sent me this in the post.' She opened her bag and took out a small jewel box. 'I always keep it in my bag, because it's the only thing of hers that I've got.' She handed her the box. Elly struggled to open it.

'Here, let me.' Her mum took the box back. 'It's a bit stiff.' She pressed the catch and the lid shot up, revealing a silver locket on a thin silver chain.

'It's beautiful!'

'If you look on the back, you can see her name.'

Carefully, Elly picked up the locket and turned it over.

'It's her maiden name, of course,' her mum said. 'She had it before she married. My father would never have given her anything as expensive as that anyway. He'd have said it was a waste of money.'

Elly stared down at the locket.

Written on the back was a girl's name: *Rose Fairfax*.

14

So now she knew the truth. Elly looked at her reflection in her bedroom mirror. She leaned forward and breathed a circle on the glass. Wrote *Rose Fairfax* with her index finger. Sat back and stared at the misty face with its scared wide-eyed expression. Her gran was a Fairfax. That meant she was part Fairfax too. The link between past and present. It was the last thing she'd imagined. Now she knew why she had felt so close to Eleanor Fairfax, why she could think her thoughts, feel what she felt. It was not coincidence. The other link must be her relationship with Hugh. Morton and Fairfax. A symmetrical pattern. That had to be why the past was re-enacting itself. She was the catalyst. She had started it. Maybe that was why she alone saw the figures.

Elly ran her fingers through her hair. It crackled with static electricity. She stared into the mirror, allowed her thoughts to drift. Funny how when she caught sight of herself, she just saw a familiar, ordinary person: Elly Laverty. And her dad. When she looked at him, he was just her dad. She didn't see what others saw, the colour of his skin, her skin. Black, white. Did it matter? It shouldn't. But deep down, Elly knew that it did. It mattered a lot. The colour of her skin made her different. That was why Jessica Thornton bullied her. She'd seen it in her eyes, the way she looked her up and down so coolly, then looked away. And it was also what she saw in her form-teacher's eyes when she'd asked her to stay back after school for a 'chat'. Elly let her mind to go back to that time, remembering how her heart had lifted. Somebody had noticed her pain. Something was going to be done to help her.

The 'chat' had happened the same day as the phone call about Aunt Rose. If she closed her eyes, Elly could see her classroom clearly: tables, whiteboard, lockers, and her teacher standing stiffly behind her desk, arms folded. She had looked Elly up and down, without smiling, then looked away. Stupid, stupid, Elly thought, shaking her head. How had she failed to read her body language?

'I understand you seem to be having some problems with the rest of the group,' the teacher had said.

Eagerly, Elly opened her mouth to explain about Jessica. The name-calling, the lies, the way she'd been pushed out of everything. But she had been cut off mid-sentence.

'I gather you are creating a bad atmosphere.'

'Huh?' Elly's mouth fell open.

'I've had a lot of complaints from other students, Elrose. They all say the same thing: that they've tried to be friendly to you but you are prickly and unpleasant. You go out of your way to cause trouble. Can you tell me why this is?'

'But . . . I . . . ' Elly felt the words draining away.

'I'm not going to discuss this, Elrose. I want you to think very carefully about the way you behave towards others. This has always been a pleasant form and I'm not going to let somebody like you destroy it.'

Elly stared at the woman's cold, unresponsive, shut-in face. She was so shocked that she didn't know whether to laugh or cry.

'Now, I'm willing to give you the opportunity to put things right. If you want to be part of the group, you're going to have to make some changes. For a start, you're going to have to work on your attitude problem. Do I make myself quite clear?'

Elly felt as if her inside was frozen.

'Do you hear me, Elrose?'

Elly nodded, looking away. She wouldn't break down, wouldn't cry. Wouldn't give them the satisfaction of winning.

'Good. You may go now.'

I will survive this, she remembered thinking. I won't fall apart.

Elly opened her eyes again, got up from the chair, crossed to the bedroom window. The early-summer breeze ruffled the net curtains. She listened. The sound of a lawnmower two gardens down. Someone calling a child's name. In the distance, beyond the row of cottages, the wood was silent. She shivered. She had to stop returning to the past. Her past, Eleanor's past. Shadowy fragments in the mirror of her mind. She had to erase them from her memory. She must start living in the present. She glanced at her watch. She ought to make a phone call. Apologize to Hugh. Maybe ask him over tomorrow. If the call went well. Damage limitation. But first, she needed to think up some sort of an explanation. The truth, but not the whole truth. She wasn't going to reveal that she was related to a possible murderer. Especially when the victim was a member of his family. It was not a basis for an ongoing friendship. And then she had to prepare herself to meet 'Aunt Rose'.

'Maybe your dad was right,' Elly's mum said thoughtfully. She turned into the hospital car park. 'Perhaps it would have been better if I'd just come out with it and told you who Aunt Rose really was.'

116

'Dad?' Elly turned to look at her. 'When did you talk to Dad?'

'The other night. You were in bed.'

No, she wasn't. Elly remembered sitting on the cold landing. Listening in the dark to their voices. The conversation she'd thought was about splitting up.

'I thought there'd be a right moment,' her mum murmured. 'But there wasn't, was there? I should have listened to him.' She reversed the car into a vacant space.

'Mum . . . ' Elly began. She wanted to seize the moment. To ask about Dad. The future, their future. To see if there was one.

'Mmmm?'

'Nothing.' The words wouldn't come. Would there ever be a right moment for this? she thought.

'Right, are you set?'

Elly licked her dry lips. Nodded.

Elly had lingered in the hospital corridor, trying to prolong the moment when she would have to go into the ward. She had been scared. Scared of what her gran might look like, scared of how she would react. But in the event, she need not have worried. As soon as the nurse showed them into the ward, she had forgotten her fear and followed her mum over to the bed by the window, where the old lady was waiting, propped up against a couple of pillows. Elly had taken one look into her eyes—Fairfax eyes, looking straight up at her with such love and longing—and had been filled with compassion.

'Elrose . . . '

'Hello, Gran,' she'd whispered, smiling. She'd sat down on the bed and taken the delicate, paper-thin hands into her own. They hadn't talked much—Elly's mum had done most of the talking, but her gran had never taken her eyes from Elly's face, as if she were trying to memorize every little detail of her features. And her eyes had followed Elly as she and her mum walked down the ward at the end of visiting-time.

'Will she be coming home soon?' Elly asked on the way home. Her gran had looked very ill. There were alarming tubes strapped to her wrist and a monitoring machine bleeped constantly, flashing geometric patterns on to a screen.

'I don't know,' her mum said. 'There seem to be some complications.'

'Oh?' Elly picked up on the worry in her voice.

'I spoke to the nurse. She says they're going to do some tests tomorrow. Perhaps we'll know a bit more then.'

'She must be missing Flossy.'

'I think she is.'

'Maybe we could bring her in some time.'

'If they allow dogs in, we could.'

They drove in silence for a while.

'If she doesn't come home for a long time,' Elly was following a train of thought, 'what will happen to Flossy?'

Her mum shook her head. 'I don't know.'

'Could we have her? She likes us.'

Her mum didn't reply.

'Go on, say yes,' Elly pleaded. 'She won't be any trouble. I'll walk her and feed her. And we could give her back when Gran's better.'

'It isn't that . . . ' Her mum hesitated.

'What then? You can't get rid of her, Mum, that would be completely out of order!'

'No, I wouldn't do that. It's just that I'm not sure we'll be able to take her.'

'Why not?'

'Oh dear.' Her mum suddenly sounded flustered. 'I wasn't intending to have this conversation quite yet. Not until Dad gets back. We really wanted to talk to you together.'

God! Elly's heart lurched. So there was more. 'Talk about what?' Suddenly, her voice felt croaky, her throat tight.

'It's just that Dad's job looks like being permanently based in Brussels now.'

'So?'

'So we were exploring the idea of moving.'

Elly gasped. Things swam before her eyes. 'Moving— you mean splitting up?'

'No! Of course not!' Her mum spoke indignantly. 'Whatever gave you that idea? I meant moving to Brussels—you and me. So that we can be a family again.'

'*Move abroad?*'

'*Possibly* move abroad. We haven't decided. As I said, we wanted to talk it through with you.'

'But . . . your business?' Elly stammered. She was in total shock. This was not an option she'd considered.

'I can run it from anywhere,' her mum said. 'All I need is a computer and a phone. And England is only a couple of hours away now.'

'But that would mean I'd have to leave school.' The implications were beginning to sink in.

'Yes, I know. That's why we'd have to think about it very carefully. We wouldn't want you to feel bad about leaving all your friends.'

Leaving all her friends?

Elly's mum parked the car outside the cottage, switched off the engine. 'And that's why,' she said, turning to face Elly, 'we might not be able to give Flossy a home.' She opened the car door. 'Look, let's not have a big row about this, please,' she said wearily. 'It's been a very stressful day.'

Elly felt relief flooding over her. Her parents were not getting divorced! Her nightmare had vanished into thin air. A move abroad—she'd have to leave school. Bye bye, Jessica. Row with her mum? The way she felt, she could almost have hugged her.

'Elly. Did you hear me?'

'Yeah,' Elly nodded. 'Loud and clear, Mum. Every word.'

'Brussels? Hey, go for it,' Hugh said.

'You think so?'

'It's a great city. I'd love to live there.'

Yeah, of course, he would know all about it, Elly thought wearily. She was rapidly discovering there was very little Hugh didn't know about. Or have an opinion on. It was just a tad annoying. Funny how you could really fancy somebody, she thought ruefully, then when you got to know them, little things started getting on your nerves.

Hugh reached for another digestive biscuit, dunked it into his mug of hot chocolate. 'You know, hot drinks are supposed to bring out the flavour of biscuits better than cold ones.'

'Uh-huh.'

'Especially lemonade.'

'Sorry?'

Hugh held up the soggy biscuit. 'Digestive . . . lemonade . . . doesn't work. You're not listening.'

'Yes I am,' Elly protested. 'You said Brussels was a good place to live. See.'

Hugh's face took on a patient, long-suffering expression. One more day, Elly thought, sighing inwardly. Then he'd be back at school. Trouble was she was used to her own company. The strain of having him around was already beginning to tell. Hang on in, she told herself. At least while Hugh was with her, nothing would happen. She knew that now. Whatever was going on, it was not about the Morton family. This was about the Fairfax family. About her and Eleanor.

'So,' Hugh said, 'we've done the woods. Now what?'

'I don't know. We could take Flossy for a walk across the fields. That's where I saw the family going to London.'

'Right.' Hugh set his mug down. 'Let's go.'

'Except that we haven't got the dog,' Elly went on. 'Mum's taken her in to the hospital to visit Gran.'

'So let's go on our own.'

'Please—give me a break! We've been walking round the woods all morning. I'm tired.'

'Come on, Elly,' Hugh pleaded. 'Don't wimp out. I've only got one day. I have to see them.'

Elly groaned. She was beginning to wish she'd kept her mouth shut after all. Hugh could be very persistent. She was trying not to think of it as bossy. 'Look,' she said. 'How about this: I have to get lunch for Mum and me. So say I meet you at the end of the lane at two?'

'OK,' Hugh agreed reluctantly. He got up. 'Don't go anywhere until then,' he ordered.

Elly grinned. 'OK. I won't move. So I guess you'd better see yourself out.'

But her mum didn't come back. Elly waited, then had her lunch and washed up her plate. She wrapped the rest of the sandwiches she'd made in foil. Her mum was probably still sitting by Gran's bed, talking. Laying down another stepping stone. That was how her mum had described the visits. Because so much had happened since

121

she had last seen her mother, they had been like strangers. Each visit was like a stepping stone, bridging the gap of years, gradually bringing them closer and closer to each other.

The kitchen clock ticked loudly. Elly frowned. If her mum didn't come back soon, she'd have to leave her a note. And if she didn't write the note soon, she'd be late meeting Hugh. Elly was beginning to conclude that life would be a lot safer if she spent all her time either with Hugh or here in the cottage. Of course she wanted to discover who had murdered Arbella Morton, she just didn't want to be around when she found out.

For some time, she stood in the kitchen, undecided. Then she went into the sitting-room to find some paper. She had just written '*Dear Mum*' when the phone rang shrilly right by her elbow. She jumped, picked up the receiver. 'Um . . . hello,' she began nervously, trying to remember her gran's number.

'Elly? Is that you?'

'Mum! Where are you, I've been waiting ages!'

'I'm sorry.' Mrs Laverty's voice sounded tense. 'It's Gran. She's had some sort of a stroke. Look, I don't think I shall be back for a while.'

'Oh, Mum!' Elly was instantly full of concern. 'Is she bad?'

There was a pause at the other end of the line. 'She's not too good, Elly. The doctors are with her now.'

'Don't worry, Mum, I'm on my way.' Elly put down the phone, screwed up the half-written note. She grabbed her bag, was through the front door, moving on automatic pilot before it hit her: how on earth was she going to get to the hospital? She checked her wallet. Not enough for a taxi. She had a little money—enough perhaps for her bus fare. But was there a bus to the hospital and if so, where did it go from? For a moment, she stood helplessly on the front step. Then she thought of Helen Morton. Surely she would help.

Elly set off up the road at a run.

At the top of the lane, she turned right and began to run along the narrow country road that led to Helen Morton's cottage. Desperation gave her extra stamina and she sped on, praying that she would get to the house quickly, that Helen Morton would be in.

It was only a few minutes, although it seemed like ages, until she saw the familiar bend in the road. Elly raced the last fifty yards and turned the corner, hope high in her heart.

The cottage had gone. In its place, tall trees stood like sentinels barring her way.

No! Elly's brain screamed. *Not now!*

There was the sound of running feet behind her. Elly spun round and saw Eleanor Fairfax coming straight towards her. Her cap was askew, her face bright red, her eyes almost starting out of her head. Elly tried to get out of her way. Too late. Eleanor did not appear to see her, and anyway, she was running much too fast to stop. Without the slightest change in her expression or her pace, Eleanor Fairfax ran straight into her.

Elly heard the thud; she felt the impact.

Then everything took on a slow, dreamlike quality.

15

In the silky purple twilight, Eleanor Fairfax was running. Her bare feet hardly made any sound upon the cool grass. She had hitched up her long skirt and discarded her clumsy shoes ages ago. She had to get to Morton House. She had to warn them before it was too late.

Eleanor's breath was coming in great sobbing gasps. Her heart was pounding in her chest. Her hair blew around her face and into her mouth and eyes, but she paid it no heed. She was God's instrument, chosen to save them from certain death. Fear gave wings to her feet. Nothing could stop her.

It was pure chance that she had overheard the conversation between the men, as she stopped outside the strange house to swap her heavy basket from one arm to the other. The upstairs window was open and as she leaned against the wall, she had heard their voices. At first, she didn't really listen, then all at once, she recognized one of the speakers. The name 'Morton' jumped out at her and suddenly she became very still, ears strained to catch every word of their conversation.

'He writes that he is trying to get them out of the city by night.' The voice was that of Samuel Leyburn, Hugh Morton's steward. 'He wants me to make ready the house for their arrival.'

'He is sending them here? He must be mad!'

'When will they come?'

'Tonight, maybe. If all goes well.'

'They will bring the Sickness with them!'

'Nay, he writes that they do not have it.'

'But it will come with them—it will be in their clothes, in the air around them!'

'You must send him word. They shall not come!'

'It would be too late, my friends. He writes that he already has the marks upon him. He will not be long for this world. Probably dead already.'

There was a pause.

'So he is not coming?'

'Just the boy and the girl?'

Another pause, longer this time.

'Then we know what we must do!'

'Aye, it is our duty to protect our fellow men!'

'We must rid the village of this evil Pestilence that would come upon us to slay us all!'

'And there is more, my friends,' Samuel Leyburn's normally calm voice had an edge of barely suppressed excitement, 'for he writes that they will be carrying . . . '

But Eleanor never heard what it was they would be carrying, for just then a wagon went by, and drowned out the voices. When it had passed, the room above was silent. The men had gone.

Now she saw the house, its roof and chimneys outlined darkly against the purple sky. Her heart throbbed, for there was the big black mare, its white blaze showing up clearly in the dusky twilight. He was here! Hugh Morton was here. There was not a minute to lose.

'Hugh, Hugh!' Eleanor cried, gasping for breath. She ran through the open front door.

The house was in total darkness. All the servants had gone, each to his own home or village, all terrified of catching the Sickness, but Eleanor knew her way, even in the blackness. She crossed the great hall and felt with her outspread hands for the door handle on the far side.

Turning it, she mounted the stairs, one hand flat against the cold wall to steady her progress, until she came to the top, and stepped out onto the long gallery.

The air smelt musty and stale. For a brief moment, Eleanor stood there, in the thick fetid darkness, wondering where Hugh was. Then, she heard a faint sound and saw the flickering light of a candle under the door of Arbella's room, and in an instant, she was there, fearlessly opening the door, stepping inside the room, a joyous greeting upon her lips.

He was standing by the half-open window, staring out at the darkening sky, a slim figure wearing his familiar green breeches and doublet, hatless, his hair streaming like moonlight upon his slender shoulders.

'Hugh,' she whispered, and at the sound of her voice, the figure whirled round and as she caught sight of the face, Eleanor gasped, her hands flying to her mouth in shock.

It was Arbella Morton!

'But . . . I . . . I . . . '

'You . . . you,' Arbella mocked, striding over towards her. 'What are *you* doing here, Eleanor Fairfax? *Why* is the house not ready to welcome us? *And where is Samuel Leyburn, my father's steward?*' She gripped Eleanor by the arm, and shook her imperiously. 'Answer me, girl!' she shouted. Her eyes narrowed ominously.

'I . . . you . . . he . . . ' Eleanor stuttered, temporarily lost for words.

'Well? What ails you? Are you moonstruck or something?' Arbella cried.

'I thought you were . . . '

'You thought I was Hugh, didn't you?' Arbella permitted herself a small, triumphant smile. She released Eleanor, stood back and stared at her. Eleanor was suddenly painfully aware that she was red in the face and puffing like a pair of bellows. Her bodice was soaked in sweat and the hem of her dress was thick with mud. She sensed Arbella's disgust.

'Ninny!' Arbella scoffed. 'Do you think a girl can ride safely through the countryside in times like these, when the roads are thick with robbers and cut-purses and worse? That is why I am disguised as a boy.'

'Then where is Hugh?' Eleanor asked, finding her tongue at last.

A strange, sad expression flitted across Arbella's face as she answered, 'He is nearby. He will join me shortly.' For a second her face fell, losing its brightness and animation, then she turned upon Eleanor again. 'But you have not said what you are doing here, Eleanor Fairfax,' she snapped. 'I thought you had gone to Amwell to live with your brother.'

'I had gone, but I came back to deliver some lace that I had made. Oh, Arbella,' Eleanor cried, remembering her mission at last, 'you must both flee! Samuel Leyburn has betrayed you, and even now he and some other men are looking for you to kill you.'

Arbella staggered back as if she had been struck. The colour drained from her face, so that her eyes looked like blue ice-crystals against the whiteness of her skin.

'Is this true?' she whispered. 'But why?'

'They say you bring the Sickness with you,' Eleanor said simply.

For a moment, Arbella remained motionless, taking in what Eleanor had said. Then she abruptly turned on her heel, strode over to the bed and started rummaging through the piles of clothes that she had thrown upon it. She began to divide them methodically into piles, muttering to herself. Helpless, Eleanor stood by and watched her, expecting to hear at any moment the sound of hoofbeats on the drive and the rough voices of the men outside the house.

127

'What are you doing?' she ventured finally.

Arbella looked up at her, a puzzled expression upon her face, almost as if she had forgotten that Eleanor was still in the room.

'I am sorting out the clothes that I shall need for our journey,' she said calmly and resumed her task.

'What journey?'

'The journey we must make, my brother and I. It was always in my mind that we would not stay here—the memories are too powerful and I do not think that he . . . we could bear to live on in the house now that our parents and our brothers and sisters are all dead.'

'But where will you go?'

'To France,' Arbella said firmly. 'We will ride for the coast tonight and take ship first thing in the morning.'

'But what about me?' Eleanor cried.

'You? What have you to do with our plans?' Arbella exclaimed indignantly. 'You are nothing to us. Nothing at all.'

'Hugh made me a promise,' Eleanor said. 'He promised that when he returned from London, we should be betrothed.'

'What!' Arbella started back, as if she had received a shock. 'When did Hugh say this?'

'He wrote to me.'

'I don't believe you!' Arbella cried, colour flooding back into her cheeks. 'You are lying—my brother Hugh betrothed to a peasant? It is quite impossible! And how could he write to you—why, you cannot read!'

'I can make out a few words,' Eleanor answered defensively. She fumbled in the bodice of her dress and produced a damp, crumpled sheet of paper. She held it out and Arbella snatched it from her hand. '*Dearest and Sweetest Eleanor*' she read aloud, then suddenly she screamed, '*No!*' She flung the letter away from her as if the paper had suddenly burst into flames. It fluttered to the floor, like a bird with broken wings.

'So you see,' Eleanor quietly bent down and retrieved her letter, 'I was not lying.'

For a few seconds Arbella stared at her, hands clenched, her eyes pin-points of fury. Then she turned abruptly, buried her face in a pile of clothing and burst into loud, jagged sobs.

'It cannot be,' she sobbed, 'and even if it is true, Hugh will never marry anybody. Not now!'

Eleanor went over and stood by the bed, looking down at the shaking yellow curls and the thin, heaving shoulders. Something was terribly wrong. 'Arbella,' she asked quietly, 'where is Hugh?'

Arbella raised her tear-stained face. Again, the same strange sad expression crossed her flushed features. 'He is nearby,' she repeated mechanically, not meeting Eleanor's eye.

'Then should not we go and warn him of the danger?'

'There is no point. He would not understand.' Arbella spoke dully. 'You see, my beloved brother—the Hugh that wrote you that letter—is not the same Hugh any more.'

Eleanor felt fear clutch cold-fingered at her heart. 'He has the Sickness?' she whispered dry-mouthed, her eyes wide with horror.

'No, though I have wished over and over again that he had. It would have been better and kinder that way. It is a thousand times worse.' Arbella sat up, struggled to steady her voice. She gripped her hands together so hard that the knuckles went white. 'You see, he has seen the Sickness take hold of our family, one by one. He has seen them die slowly and agonizingly: mother, brothers, sister, father, until only he and I were left alone in that terrible, stinking house of death. He has never been strong like me. After a while, he could not bear it any longer.'

'I do not understand,' Eleanor faltered, bewildered.

'His mind is gone,' Arbella said with a sob. 'Poor Hugh. He does not know anything or anyone. He still thinks our parents are alive. He talks to them. He is resting in the stables now. I could not bring him into the house for fear that he would go completely mad with grief. That is why I must get him away to France. I know that a change of scene will cure him.'

'Then I must come with you,' Eleanor cried, horrified. 'I can nurse him back to health. And I can work with my hands to make a little money for us to live by. Please, Arbella, let me go with you—there is nothing left for me here now.'

Arbella shook her head. 'You have your father and your family,' she said. 'What would they say if you did not return to them?' She smiled grimly. 'And we have money enough, believe me. We do not need to sponge off you.'

'My father is no longer here. He has always wanted to go to the New World to start afresh. Now, after the new laws against our religion . . . ' Eleanor's voice faltered, ' . . . and my brothers do not want me—I am only in the way and another mouth to feed. I have no one in this world but Hugh. Let me go with you. I beg you.'

Silence.

Arbella looked very thoughtful, head on one side. 'So there is nobody here who would miss you?' she said slowly, staring at Eleanor as if the germ of an idea was gradually forming in her brain.

'Nobody.'

'And yet . . . ' Arbella got to her feet and walked over to the window, speaking as if to herself and in such a low undertone that Eleanor couldn't really follow what she was saying. ' . . . and yet could I bear to share my beloved Hugh with another? Never! But what if she stays? She is stupid. If they question her hard, will she not let slip my plans? I do not want her with me but I do not want her away from me. So what remedy?'

There was a long pause. Eleanor waited breathlessly for Arbella's answer. Finally, Arbella seemed to reach a decision. She suddenly turned round, and came towards Eleanor with a gay smile upon her face just like in the old days, when they were children growing up and playing together.

'Well, Eleanor,' she smiled, 'perhaps you shall come with us after all—but,' she went on, holding up a warning hand as Eleanor broke into a profusion of thanks, 'you cannot travel in those rags. Here, I will find you something proper to wear—after all, you are going to France.' Arbella went and rummaged through the pile of dresses, finally pulling one out from the bottom of the heap and holding it up in front of her. 'Yes, this one will do! You must put this on. See—it is a lovely dress. Red velvet. Hugh's favourite colour. It will cheer him to see you in it. Be quick now and take off that dreadful skirt.'

Obediently, Eleanor stripped off her clothes and put on the soft, luxurious dress. It was a little tight under the arms and a trifle long in the skirt, but it fitted her well enough. She picked up Hugh's precious letter and replaced it in the new bodice, tucking it securely down next to her heart.

'I am ready now,' she said calmly.

There was another pause whilst Arbella studied her carefully, from head to toe. Then she shook her head. 'But you have no shoes,' she said, shocked. 'You cannot travel barefoot. Go over to the chest and look inside. I am sure there is a pair of good leather shoes in there somewhere.'

Eleanor went and stooped down over the big wooden chest. 'It is too dark, I cannot see anything,' she said.

'Let me bring the candle over,' Arbella said. She came and stood close behind Eleanor. 'Now, why don't you bend down and have a really good look,' she said very quietly.

Eleanor bent over the chest and as she did so, Arbella suddenly set down the candle, grabbed her by the waist and pushed her into the chest. It all happened so quickly that Eleanor did not have time to resist. Arbella caught hold of the heavy wooden lid and slammed it down.

Muffled noises came from within the chest, but Arbella ignored them. Humming a little tune, as if nothing unusual had occurred, she picked up a pile of dresses, thrust them into a travelling bag and walked to the door. At the threshold she paused, candle in hand.

'I shouldn't bother to scream,' she said calmly. 'There is nobody to hear you.'

Then she went out, taking the candle and shutting the door behind her.

16

It was pitch black inside the chest. For a while Eleanor lay on her side just as she had fallen, completely stunned. Her ears were still ringing with the sound of the great lid slamming down, so that her brain seemed unable to comprehend what had happened to her.

Then, as the ringing sound faded away, to be replaced by total silence, it came to her that this must be some kind of joke. *'Arbella?'* she queried. Then louder, *'Hugh?'* but nobody answered. They must be hiding, Eleanor thought. All she had to do was lie here for a while longer, then the chest would be unlocked, the lid thrown up and there they would be, two laughing faces looking down at her, chiding her for being afraid, and she'd rise and step lightly out of the chest. Then they'd all leave the room and go down the wide oak staircase together and there would be a pony waiting for her outside. Hugh would help her mount it and then they would be off, galloping through the night until they got to France.

Eleanor did not know where France was exactly, except that it was far, far away from here. She had heard that the French people spoke a strange language and she suspected that they probably ate strange food as well, but she would be with Hugh and Arbella, so she would not need to be afraid of them.

Where were they?

She was beginning to feel slightly uncomfortable for she was lying in such a way that one arm was trapped under her body, whilst the other was wedged against the hard wooden side of the chest. Her legs were bent at the knee, the red velvet dress bunched awkwardly around them. Such a beautiful dress—she had never worn anything so soft. But it would be all crumpled if she stayed coiled up in the chest for much longer and she wanted to look her best for Hugh.

Poor Hugh. Eleanor felt a wave of pity engulf her. She remembered when her mother had died of a fever—how desolate and lonely she had felt. How she had lain awake at nights, missing her mother so much that it was like a pain around her heart. Hugh would need the comfort of her love and her care even more now.

Surely they must be coming soon?

It was getting hot in the chest. Eleanor could feel damp patches forming under her arms and behind her knees. Sweat started to trickle down her face. Automatically, she tried to brush it away—and discovered that she could not free her trapped arms. She struggled to release them, but only succeeded in scraping her skin painfully against the side. Suddenly, it did not feel like a joke any longer. *'Arbella!'* she shouted, over and over again, but her cries bounced back off the stout wooden walls of the chest. It was then, slowly and terrifyingly, that the truth began to dawn upon her. This was no joke.

They were not coming!

At first Eleanor could not grasp it fully. How could Arbella have deliberately left her imprisoned inside this chest, when she must know that the servants had all gone away, so that nobody would find her? How could such evil and wickedness exist in somebody so fair and beautiful? For a long while, she tried to work this out, but the air inside the chest was becoming thick and hard to breathe and it was difficult to focus her thoughts. Added to this, her cramped legs and bent arms were hurting her, and she could not stretch them out to ease her discomfort.

Eleanor started drifting in and out of consciousness. Every now and then, pain woke her up. Fear and despair kept her awake for a while and then mercifully, blankness came over her and she knew nothing until the next wave of pain woke her up again.

How long had she been lying here? she thought to herself, during one of her wakeful periods. A few hours? A day? A week? Time no longer had any form or meaning in the dark. There was only pain and horror and a desperate craving to see the sun again and breathe sweet fresh air.

And then, all at once, Eleanor saw a tiny point of light. Puzzled, she focused her eyes upon it. Why was there a light now when there was no light before, she thought groggily? She stared fixedly at the light. Where was it coming from? Had somebody come at last?

Then she realized that this light was not coming from outside the chest but was inside, there with her, and as she looked at it and wondered about it, she understood what it meant.

So this is death, Eleanor thought. Suddenly, she felt very peaceful. She began floating along a dark tunnel towards the pin-prick of light. She felt no pain, no despair, only a strange lightness in her head and body.

I am not afraid any more, she whispered to herself.

The light came towards her, growing bigger and brighter. In a little while, Eleanor thought calmly, I shall see God. I shall reach the gates of heaven and there will be my mother, with her arms open wide, waiting to welcome me in.

She moved steadily forward, and now the darkness was behind her and all the agony and the suffering were things of the past.

Light surrounded her. Light caressed and soothed her. Light bathed her in its pure radiance until her head and her body were filled with a dazzling whiteness . . .

135

17

Elly opened her eyes. She was lying on the floor, on her side. Her legs were drawn up, one arm lay underneath her. Sunlight shone through an open window straight into her face. For a split second, past and present came together in bewildering brightness.

'Where am I?' she whispered.

'Just lie still.'

Elly turned her head and looked upwards. A ring of anxious faces stared down at her. She didn't know who they were. Panic rose up inside her. Then she recognized Hugh's worried face, realized that the others were Morton House guides and visitors.

'What happened?' Elly struggled to sit up.

'Don't you remember?' Hugh asked. Elly shook her head.

'Ow, that hurts,' she exclaimed.

'I'm afraid you've given yourself a nasty bump on the head,' one of the guides said. 'Just take it easy.'

'No!' Elly struggled to a sitting position. 'I want to know what happened.'

'You knocked yourself unconscious.' The woman bent down, slipping an arm round Elly's shoulders to steady her.

Elly looked around her. She was in Arbella Morton's bedroom.

'How did it happen?'

'We were having a bit of a chat in the foyer,' one of the other guides told her. 'Suddenly, out of the blue, there you were. Gave us all such a fright! We thought it was a ghost! Anyway, you rushed in through the front door, shouting "*Hugh, Hugh!*" at the top of your voice. Then you ran straight upstairs and went into this room.'

'We followed you,' the first woman continued, 'and found you lying on the floor. You must have tripped on the edge of the carpet and banged your head on that old chest by the bed.'

'Lucky for all of us, Hugh was here. He knew just what to do.'

'Only because we'd done a first aid course at school,' Hugh admitted modestly.

'He's a real professional! First, he checked your breathing and then he put you into the recovery position,' one of the visitors explained.

So that explains why I was lying on my side, Elly thought.

'What I don't understand is why you came looking for me in the first place,' Hugh said. 'I thought we'd agreed to meet at the top of your lane.'

Elly tried to gather her thoughts together, make some sense out of them. Why had she set off from the cottage? Something must have happened before she'd become Eleanor Fairfax? Suddenly, the memories came streaming back and she remembered: *Mum, Gran!*

'I have to get to the hospital,' she cried. 'My mum's still there with Gran. I was on my way to be with them.'

'I really don't think you should be going anywhere right now.' The woman guide shook her head.

'Cup of hot sweet tea and a nice sit-down, that's the best thing,' another advised. She laid a comforting hand on Elly's arm.

'No,' Elly protested, 'you don't understand.' She shook herself free, fixed her gaze upon Hugh, sent him a frantic subliminal message: *get me out of here!*

'I think Elly might like some fresh air,' Hugh said.

'Yes, fresh air, great,' Elly agreed. 'Just what I need.' She stumbled towards the door.

'Hang on, I'm coming,' Hugh said.

Outside, the sun hit Elly in the face like a fist. She felt herself swaying, the world beginning to spin around her.

'Here.' Hugh put an arm round her, guided her to a bench. 'Put your head down between your knees for a minute.'

Meekly, Elly obeyed. She was terrified she'd pass out, return to the nightmare world she'd just left.

'God, you look awful,' Hugh commented.

'Thanks,' Elly whispered. She concentrated, filling her lungs with air, willing the nausea to subside. After a couple of long seconds, she looked up. 'I have to ring Mum,' she said. Silently, Hugh handed her his mobile. Elly dialled her mum's number.

'Elly? Where are you?' Her mother sounded anxious.

'I'm with Hugh. At Morton House. What's happening?'

'The doctors are still with Gran. Look, I don't think it's a very good idea for you to come to the hospital right now.'

'Why not?'

'Elly, I'm not supposed to use my mobile here. Can you go back home? I'll ring you when the doctors have finished.'

'I can't get in. I left my key in the kitchen,' Elly said.

'Oh, Elly!'

'You can come back with me,' Hugh said.

'Hugh says I can go back with him.'

'I think that would be a good idea. Honestly, there's nothing you can do here.'

'But I want to help you,' Elly protested.

'I'm fine, really. It would help me if you went with Hugh. Give me the phone number,' her mum said. 'I'll tell you what's happening as soon as they tell me.'

'She needs your home phone number,' Elly said. Hugh repeated it.

'Thanks. I'll phone you soon, promise.'

'Mum?' Elly queried. Then, 'She's gone.'

'Don't worry,' Hugh said. 'I'm sure everything's OK.'

Elly stared at him. Suddenly she saw in her mind another Hugh, cowering terrified in the stable. Confused and broken by what had happened. And her heart was wrung by sadness and pity so that she felt great tears welling up in her eyes.

'Elly?' Hugh said softly. 'Where are you?'

Silently, Elly shook her head.

Helen Morton carried the cup and saucer carefully into the room, placed it on a side-table.

'Now, drink this whilst it's hot,' she said. She looked down at Elly, concern on her face.

'Thanks,' Elly said.

'Are you really sure you don't want me to ring my doctor?'

'No.' Elly shook her head. 'I'll be fine.' She picked up the cup, sipped the hot sweet tea. 'Lovely, just what I need.'

'Well . . . ' Helen sighed doubtfully.

'Honestly, I'm sure.'

'Elly,' Hugh said urgently as Helen Morton went to get the rest of the drinks, 'what happened? You saw them again, didn't you?'

Elly nodded.

'So?' Hugh went on. 'You have to tell me—did you find out who murdered Arbella?'

'No,' Elly said. She placed the cup slowly onto the saucer. Her hands were shaking. 'But I found out who Arbella murdered.'

Helen Morton sat very still. Her eyes never left Elly's face. She listened intently as Elly recounted what had happened from the moment she'd left the cottage to when she'd woken up in Arbella's bedroom. Only her hands, convulsively tightening around the sides of her cup betrayed her true feelings as Elly described the tragic unfolding of the drama played out between Arbella Morton and Eleanor Fairfax.

By the time Elly had come to a faltering halt, tears were coursing freely down Helen Morton's cheeks. Hugh, his face white and shocked, was visibly shaken.

'The poor, poor girl,' Helen Morton murmured. 'There are no words, are there? Nothing to say that can alter what happened.' She shook her head slowly. 'I can't take it in. We all thought it was Arbella's body in that chest and now you tell me that it was the body of a local girl called Eleanor Fairfax.'

'And Arbella killed her!' Hugh exclaimed. 'She deliberately left her to die. That's murder!'

'I know, dear,' Helen Morton sighed, her brow furrowed with pain. 'And yet . . . somehow, I can't believe it of her. Not Arbella. She meant to return. It must have been the terrible things that happened in London that turned her brain—after all, we have to remember what she and Hugh went through. They lost their entire family—if it had happened today, they would have had counselling and therapy to get over their trauma. But they had nothing at all—just their love for each other. I'm sure it must have been an accident— such a sweet-faced innocent girl, she can't have meant to harm Eleanor!'

'Gran!' Hugh protested. 'I know you have a soft spot for Arbella, but you have to face the facts.'

'Yes. She was a vicious, deliberate, cold-blooded killer,' Elly said bleakly. 'She didn't want to share her brother with anybody else, so she killed Eleanor and then she just walked away from her crime.'

'Walked away certainly . . . but where to?' Hugh mused. 'I wonder what happened to her afterwards, and to Hugh.'

'Maybe they made it to France,' Elly said. 'But I hope not. I hope those men caught them and they got what they deserved—what she deserved, at any rate!'

'Elly!' Helen Morton said, shocked. 'What a dreadful thing to say!'

'Is it?' Elly thought of Eleanor, dying slowly and without hope in darkness and despair. She knew that the experience would haunt her for the rest of her life.

'My dear, you mustn't be so hard,' Helen Morton said gently. 'I know you've had an awful shock, and it was a terrible thing to happen, but after all, we need to remember that it all happened such a long, long time ago.'

Elly sat staring stony-faced at the table.

'Elly,' Hugh said, 'there's something you haven't told us, isn't there?'

Elly raised her head and looked at him. 'Yes, there is,' she said slowly. 'You see, I'm a Fairfax. My gran's name before she married was Rose Fairfax. I only just found out.'

Hugh gasped. Helen Morton's hands flew to her mouth as her eyes, wide and pain-filled, stared across the room at Elly.

'I'm sorry,' she whispered. 'Elly, I'm so sorry. Forgive me for being heartless. Of course, I understand now. Eleanor was somebody in your family. Of course you see it differently to us.'

'A *Fairfax*!' Hugh exclaimed. 'So all of this—it wasn't just chance then.'

Elly shook her head. 'I thought it was at first,' she said. 'I thought for a long time that it must be just coincidence.

141

But now, I believe it was Eleanor Fairfax trying to tell me what really happened to her. Only I don't know what to do now I know.'

Helen Morton didn't speak for a while. Then she said, 'There is something we must do, Hugh. We must change the headstone on that poor girl's grave for a start. Let everybody know that she isn't Arbella Morton after all, but Eleanor Fairfax.'

'I shall light a candle,' Hugh said gravely.

'So much pain and hatred,' Helen murmured. 'That poor lost girl calling across the centuries. What do you think, Elly? Can there be reconciliation between the Mortons and the Fairfaxes? Can we bury the past now and let it lie in peace?' She held out her hand. Elly hesitated, then took it.

'Thank you, Elly,' Helen Morton said. 'This is a new beginning for us and for you too.'

'Well,' Hugh said after a pause, 'that's sorted then. Only I still think it's so unfair that Elly should be the only one of us to have *seen* them.'

'What makes you think that, dear?' Helen Morton looked at him and raised her eyebrows gently.

'You mean . . . ' Hugh said slowly, '*you* saw them too?'

'Not in the same clear way as Elly,' Helen Morton said. 'But sometimes, when I was still living in the house, I felt—I don't know quite how to describe it—as if there were shadowy people walking around. I'd hear floorboards creak in upstairs room, ends of conversations, sudden laughter. I never saw them. But they always left a space where they had been, if you can understand me.'

Hugh looked puzzled but Elly nodded. 'Yes,' she said, 'I understand exactly what you mean.' *So that's why she believed me*, she thought. Somehow it didn't surprise her. Helen Morton had whatever that word was that began with 'm'. She'd felt it from their first meeting.

'Then there was the singing,' Helen went on. 'I heard that very often when I was walking in the wood.' She hummed a few bars. 'Always the same tune: "Greensleeves". I liked to think it was Arbella.'

'It was Eleanor,' Elly said.

'Was it?' Helen Morton sighed. 'Ah well. Somehow I don't think that I shall hear her any more though. Not now.'

'What will you do with the pictures, Gran?' Hugh asked. 'You're not going to keep them after this, are you? If it was me, I'd chuck them out.'

'I shall give them to the House,' Helen Morton said. 'Let them decide what to do with them. They'll probably put them on display with the other portraits. Oh dear, I don't think I shall ever be able to look at them in quite the same light again after today. To think that such a beautiful young thing could be so wicked and cruel! Well, I suppose it just goes to show that you shouldn't judge people by appearances, doesn't it?'

There was a ring at the door. Helen Morton got up slowly. Suddenly, she seemed to have aged. 'Poor Gran,' Hugh said softly. 'She's had a shock.'

Elly listened as Helen went to the door, opened it. She heard voices, a dog barking.

'It's Mum!' She leaped to her feet.

'Take it easy,' Hugh advised, but Elly was already out of the room and down the hall.

'Oh, Elly, look at that bruise on your forehead!' Her mum held her at arms length. 'What on earth happened? Are you all right?'

'I'm fine. Honestly.'

'I don't know. It's been one thing after another ever since we arrived.'

'Don't worry,' Elly said. 'It isn't going to happen any more. Promise.'

'Are you ready to go?'

'Yes.' Elly turned to Helen Morton. All at once, she felt shy, separate, didn't know what to say to her. 'Thanks for having me,' she muttered. Even to her ears, it sounded formal, cold.

'Elly!' Helen hugged her. 'You know you are always welcome here. Always.'

Elly's mum held out her hand. 'I can't thank you enough for looking after my daughter,' she said.

Helen Morton took her hand in both of her own. 'She's very special,' she said softly.

Elly followed her mum to the car. She bundled the dog into the back and slipped into the passenger seat. Helen Morton came out and stood framed in the doorway. Empathy, Elly thought. That was the word she had been searching for earlier. Helen and Hugh waved as the car pulled away. Behind them, above the green treeline, the tall brick chimneys of Morton House reached up like twisted fingers into the blue sky.

18

'Are you sure you're all right?' Elly's mum asked anxiously as they drove back.

'Fine, Mum,' Elly said firmly. It was not quite true—she was beginning to get a headache but she didn't want any more fuss. 'It was just an accident. I tripped over a carpet. Could have happened to anybody. Hey, maybe we should sue the National Trust,' she joked.

'Don't even think about it,' her mum said grimly. 'Anyway, it's not going to happen again.'

'No?'

'No. Because tomorrow we're going back home for a bit.'

'What!' Elly exclaimed. 'But I thought Gran was still bad.'

'She is and it looks like she'll be in hospital for quite a bit longer.'

'So? We should be here for her.'

'Oh, I will be,' her mum said. 'I can pop down regularly. But you've had enough time out of school. You need to get back into the routine.'

'I don't mind.'

'I'm sure you don't,' her mum said drily. 'But I do. So tomorrow we'll go back.'

'Hey, what about when we move to Brussels?' Elly exclaimed. 'We can't leave Gran on her own.'

'We're not moving tomorrow,' her mum said. 'There's a lot of thinking and sorting to do first. And when she's better, we'll see what Gran wants to do. Meanwhile, let's take things one step at a time.'

'We're not going to leave Flossy here are we?'

'No. We'll take her with us.'

'Really? Hey, great!'

'I'm glad you feel like that, because you're going to have to look after her.' Her mum shot her a sideways glance. 'Like you promised . . . '

'Right.' Elly pulled a face. The prospect of early morning walks stretched a little unappetizingly ahead. They drew up outside the cottage.

'It'll give you something to do,' her mum remarked, switching off the engine. 'I feel you've had a rather boring time over the last week or so.'

Elly opened her mouth to protest. Shut it again. There was no point. Her mum would never understand. Never, never. Best to leave her happy in her delusion. She got out of the car.

Later that evening, Elly mounted the narrow stairs, pushed open the door to her bedroom. She wouldn't do this again, she thought. Tomorrow she'd be home. The next day, she'd be back in school. To her surprise, she found the idea did not terrify her. She was even relishing the prospect of seeing Jessica and her gang again. She had scores to settle, debts to collect. It was pay-back time. Elly wasn't sure what she was going to do, but she was confident that she'd know when the time came. It was not going to be like before. She had changed, moved on. She had gone with Eleanor to the rim where death and life meet. And had returned. Inside, she was stronger, no longer fearful.

Smiling to herself, Elly put on her baggy T-shirt, went over to the window. It was a cloudless evening, the sky dark and star-studded with a full moon like a silver saucer riding high. She looked up at it for a while, wondering how often Eleanor Fairfax had stood at the window of her cottage, staring up at the same moon and thinking about her future. She got the box of matches she'd brought upstairs with her, lit the small candle she'd carried up with it and placed it in a saucer. *'This is for you, Eleanor,'* she said. She put the candle in the window.

Then she got into bed and stretched herself down under the duvet.

The next morning, Elly carried her case downstairs and left it by the front door. She went into the kitchen, filled a bowl with cornflakes, added milk and took it into the front room. Her mum was wiping down surfaces, collecting up bits and pieces. Already, the cottage was beginning to resume its solitary atmosphere.

'You missed Hugh,' her mum told her. 'He rang earlier to say goodbye.'

'Oh?' Elly stirred her cornflakes. Tried to look nonchalant. She'd been thinking about Hugh, regretting that they hadn't said goodbye properly. She'd wondered whether she would ever see him again.

Her mum handed her a piece of paper. 'That's where he goes to school.'

Elly glanced down at it. 'Uh-huh.'

'And his mobile phone number and his e-mail address.' She gave Elly a sly look. 'I think he wants you to stay in touch.'

Elly folded the paper, put it in her pocket. 'I might,' she said non-committally.

'Oh, Elly! He's such a nice boy.'

Elly rolled her eyes, groaned loudly. Her mum didn't change. Still the same high cringe factor. Tragic. 'I think I'll just go upstairs,' she said, getting up. 'Don't want to leave anything important.'

The small back bedroom looked bare and remote. Elly checked it over. She'd missed nothing. Everything was packed. There was no sign that she'd ever been there. She felt the memory of her was already fading away. She looked around for the very last time, remembering how she had lain awake last night, watching the candle as it flickered bravely against the night sky, across the infinity of time between past and present. And in its flame, she'd seen peace and hope and the promise of a bright new future.

'Are you ready to go?' her mum shouted up.

'Ready,' Elly called back. She ran quickly downstairs, got into the car and closed the door. She fastened her seat belt. And when car set off down the lane, she did not look back.

Also by Carol Hedges

Bright Angel
ISBN 0 19 271898 3

Bryn knew, with fierce certainty, that his dad's death had not been the result of a 'freak accident at work' . . . Somebody had deliberately and cold-bloodedly arranged his death. Bryn was determined to find out who had killed him and why.

Bryn has never bothered much about politics and how the world is run. After all, it is the end of the twenty-second century, and the world is at peace, ruled by the President and the global companies. But when his dad dies in mysterious circumstances in his laboratory at Globechem, Bryn begins to ask questions.

And Bryn is not the only one to question the way things are: Jade has always felt an outsider, able to see and feel things other people can't and plagued by a sense of foreboding and visions of apocalypse. When she and Bryn get together, they realize that things are not always what they seem, that the world may not be perfect after all . . . and that they are in terrible danger.

Jigsaw
ISBN 0 19 275171 9

Chaos theory . . . Events that seem random always have a reason for happening, even if we don't understand it at the time. For instance, a black car passes a cyclist on a rainy evening. A boy dies. The connection?

Annie has always been an outsider in her English school. Uprooted from her home in Norway when her parents split up, she has never felt accepted by her peers; and one of her chief tormenters was Grant Penney, always the first to tease her about her 'Viking ancestors' and her 'funny accent'. But when Grant commits suicide, Annie feels compelled to try to find out what had driven such an outwardly confident and brash person to such despair. As the pieces of the jigsaw finally fall into place, Annie is forced to realize that maybe she and Grant had more in common than she thought.

Other Oxford fiction

The War Orphan
Rachel Anderson
ISBN 0 19 275095 X

'You can't say anything can you? You know nothing. You are nothing. You are a dot. You are one of a hundred thousand homeless children. You are just a casualty of war.'

Once Simon had thought he was in control of his life. But what is the story he keeps hearing in his head? Is it his own? Or does it belong to the child who his parents claim is his brother—Ha, the war orphan?

Simon is becoming obsessed by the fascination, the horror, and all engulfing reality of total war.

The Scavenger's Tale
Rachel Anderson
ISBN 0 19 275022 4

It is 2015, after the great Conflagration, and London has become a tourist sight for people from all over the world, coming to visit the historic Heritage Centres. These are out of bounds to people like Bedford and his sister Dee who live in an Unapproved Temporary Dwelling and have to scavenge from skips and bins just to stay alive.

Bedford begins to notice something odd about the tourists: when they arrive in the city, they are desperately ill, but when they leave they seem to have been miraculously cured. And then the Dysfuncs start disappearing. It is only when a stranger appears, terribly injured, that Bedford begins to put two and two together . . .

The Stones are Hatching

Geraldine McCaughrean

ISBN 0 19 275091 7

'You are the one,' he said. 'You must go. You must stop the Worm waking. You must save us.'

Phelim was the only one, they said, the only one who could save the world from the Hatchlings of the Stoor Worm. The Stoor Worm, who had been asleep for aeons, was beginning to waken. The dreadful sounds of war had roused it, and now its Hatchlings were abroad, terrorizing the people who had forgotten all about them, forgotten all the ancient magics.

But how could Phelim, who was only a boy, after all, save the world from all these dreadful monsters? And where could he find the Maiden, the Fool, and the Horse who were supposed to help him? As Phelim leaves his home and sets out on his quest, the words ring in his ears: 'You are the one. To stop the Worm waking. To do what must be done.'

Prove Yourself a Hero

K. M. Peyton

ISBN 0 19 275088 7

The hands descended on his face, suffocating him, stifling his screams with mouthfuls of woollen windings and mufflings until he could feel all the panic, literally stuffed down his throat, exploding in his breast. He was out of control and knew it, fighting with his own terror which he knew was more dangerous in the confined space than anything further that his assailants could do to him.

In this tense and thrilling novel, K. M. Peyton's narrative gives the reader an illuminating insight into the behaviour of different people under stress—the victim, those who care about him, and those who are inflicting harm on him.

Chandra
Frances Mary Hendry

ISBN 0 19 275058 5
Winner of the Writer's Guild Award and the Lancashire Book Award

Chandra can't believe her luck. The boy her parents have chosen for her to marry seems to be modern and open-minded. She's sure they will have a wonderful life together. So once they are married she travels out to the desert to live with him and his family—only when she gets there, things are not as she imagined.

Alone in her darkened room she tries to keep her strength and her identity. She is Chandra and she won't let it be forgotten.

River Boy
Tim Bowler

ISBN 0 19 275035 6
Winner of the Carnegie Medal

Standing at the top of the fall, framed against the sky, was the figure of a boy. At least, it looked like a boy, though he was quite tall and it was hard to make out his features against the glare of the sun. She watched and waited, uncertain what to do, and whether she had been seen.

When Jess's grandfather has a serious heart attack, surely their planned trip to his boyhood home will have to be cancelled? But Grandpa insists on going so that he can finish his final painting, 'River Boy'. As Jess helps her ailing grandfather with his work, she becomes entranced by the scene he is painting. And then she becomes aware of a strange presence in the river, the figure of a boy, asking her for help and issuing a challenge that will stretch her swimming talents to the limits. But can she take up the challenge before it is too late for Grandpa . . . and the River Boy?

It's My Life
Michael Harrison

ISBN 0 19 275042 9

As soon as he opens his front door, Martin feels that something's wrong. But he never expects the hand over his mouth, the rope around his wrists, and the mysterious man who's after a large ransom. Before Martin knows it, he's a pawn in a dangerous game that becomes more and more terrifying with every turn . . .